More from the author

Visit: www.callumpbrown.com

To listen to the audiobook version of this book, links are available at the website.

For illustration enquiries

Email: jillianharrison4@gmail.com

The Unexpected Joys
of Being a Pigeon

Callum Brown

For Mum and Dad

For some of us, books are as important as almost anything else on earth. What a miracle it is that out of these small, flat, rigid squares of paper unfolds world after world after world, worlds that sing to you, comfort and quiet or excite you. Books help us understand who we are and how we are to behave. They show us what community and friendship mean; they show us how to live and die.

Anne Lamott

1

The morning after his mum had her accident, Paddy realised he had to look after himself from now on. He was actually pretty well prepared for independence – he just didn't know it yet.

His training for a life alone began shortly after he was born. Paddy's dad, Patrick Senior, flew the nest as soon as he had taught his son how to fly, which left young Paddy and his mum to fend for themselves.

You see, Patrick Senior was a top-class racing pigeon, so spent most of his adult life away from home, working with a trainer, flying as fast and as far as he could.

At around the time the little chick Paddy was born, Patrick Senior was facing increasing pressure from his team to dedicate more and more hours to practice. He was his trainer's most prized asset; a rising star of the racing circuit, and a heart-throb to boot. When he was offered a shiny new contract, which promised a lifetime supply of grain, seeds and berries, he accepted in an instant. The deal also included a countryside bird mansion, complete with three butlers, two chefs and a Swedish masseuse. He acquired the nickname 'fancy pigeon' because of the special perks he received, such as wing massages and a hot bird bath every night.

However, instead of sharing the profits with his wife and Paddy at the home nest in London, he chose to banquet every night with a harem of lady pigeons in his private quarters. In the glamorous and fiercely competitive world of professional bird sport, there is hardly place for family.

Leaving home allowed Patrick Senior to train harder than ever, and he rapidly rose to the top of the world rankings. In the process, he made use of his lifetime supply of grain, and became stupendously fat. He was also rumoured to have acquired a taste for more intoxicating substances, namely petrol, and was apparently even seen loitering in garage forecourts late at night, slurping up spillages. The less said about that the better.[1]

In any case, when Paddy's mum heard what Patrick Senior had been up to away from home, she resorted to emptying all of his belongings into the sewers, and put up a barricade around her nest, so that even if he wanted to come back one day, he couldn't. That, as they say, was the end of that.

---

[1] This story is still to be corroborated by official bird news but it's been the tweet of the town for some time. For the uninitiated, birdy gossip is usually exchanged via the following news outlets: *The Avian Post*, *The Truth is Hard to Swallow*, and *The Daily Chirp*.

In truth though, everyone (well, everyone except Paddy and his mum) worshipped Patrick Senior. Half the birds in London wanted to be him, and the other half wanted to share a nest with him. He was a global sensation, and the fans loved his playboy lifestyle.

He was becoming the fastest, fattest, probably drunkest pigeon in England, and in the bird world at least, that's pretty damn cool.

Patrick Senior had his own unique racing number too, which all of his fans knew by heart: R02390. It was a fancy title for a fancy pigeon, but it didn't really mean anything. Paddy inherited this number as his surname, making him Patrick Jr. R02390, which is the bird name equivalent of being the son of a lord. Everyone was jealous of Paddy when he was growing up, but he always said it didn't make him any different. Even though he was the son of the most famous racing pigeon in the country, he didn't *feel* particularly special having a dad that was never home.

That said, his dad's fame did work to his advantage for a while. He used to tell the other birds his age how his dad, Patrick Senior, king of the skies and superstar racer, taught him how to fly. Paddy shared his dad's tips on flying technique so that all his friends could all go faster, and this made Paddy the most sought after pigeon in the nest at one point.

As time passed though, and as he saw less and less of his dad, Paddy ran out of interesting stories to tell, so naturally became less popular. Eventually, his friends started to doubt whether he really was Patrick Senior's son after all. Paddy found himself spending more and more time alone.

Yet Paddy didn't really have much time to feel sorry for himself, because the second major part of his preparation for a solitary life was caring for his Mum, who was also famous. She was always getting in trouble too, but for different reasons.

Sometimes known as Matilda the magnificent, more commonly known as MTM, Paddy's mum was one of the most daring birds ever to have graced the streets of London. She took part in the highly dangerous pigeon sport of poop flying, which involves doing one's business at top speed, aiming to hit moving objects in the city (cars, cyclists, double-decker buses, grannies on wheels; you name it, a pigeon has most likely pooped on it). The sport requires immense bravery, tenacity and crucially, a voracious appetite. Nobody can poop that much on empty stomach.

MTM was a three-time national poop champion (in the aerial acrobatics class), and had recently been awarded a lifetime achievement prize at the prestigious annual pigeon ceremony, 'the Poopies'. She won her silver Poopy award, which is a real poop wrapped in tin foil[2], for her long career of death-defying stunts. In the aerial acrobatics class,

---

[2] Dog poop is preferred as it is the most readily available type of poop in London. That said, the consistency is often variable. Some of the more provincial award-dos use fox poo or rabbit droppings as they tend to hold the foil better.

points are awarded for spins, flips, near misses and extended upside-down flight. Mid-flight poops guarantee a score multiplier. The more insane the routine, the better the score.

Not only was she devastatingly effective, she performed her moves with unparalleled style and grace too. Many described her as an artist rather than acrobat.

Her signature move was a triple-somersault triple-poo, which resulted in a direct hit on 3 consecutive vehicles. It was an astonishing trick in itself, but it wasn't enough for MTM. She dreamed of one day doing a quadruple (4 spins, 4 poos, 4 vehicles), but in training, every time she tried it, she fell and injured herself.

She was a stubborn and determined pigeon, so attempted the feat many times, which required a huge amount of Paddy's care and attention, and needless to say, a hell of a lot of food. This meant that Paddy was the one making the nest, endlessly topping up the mountain of food scraps and generally keeping everything in order, so that his mum could get ready for her next attempt.

As MTM reached the twilight of her career, each of her stunts had been getting crazier with every tournament. Commentators speculated that she was fuelled by her resentment of Patrick Senior, which may have been true. Paddy tried to get his mum to stop, but she was never satisfied, always seeking perfection. She was an adrenaline junkie too, and this worried Paddy.

Growing up with famous parents should have been cool, but it was stressful business for Paddy. His "friends" just wanted to get close to his parents, and actually, so did he.

MTM's final stunt, 'The Death Wish', would be her most outlandish yet, and her masterpiece: the culmination of years of dedication and artistry. It would be at the 'Poopfest Games', in front of thousands of adoring fans. The Games take place every 4 years, so this would be her farewell on the big stage.

Paddy pleaded that this would be his mother's last attempt at the fabled quadruple-somersault quadruple-poo. She said that it would.

When she outlined the routine to Paddy in the buildup to the event, even he had to admit it was impressive:

The Death Wish – choreographed and performed by MTM

Step 1: Fly upside down over an oncoming bus
Step 2: Find a pizza delivery rider and swoop down onto their helmet
Step 3: Take first poo, on helmet
Step 4: Backflip onto pizza box on back of delivery rider's bike
Step 5: Steal a piece of pizza (this mid-move snack is essential to maximise the number of poops during flight)

Step 6: Begin flying forwards at top speed, curving upwards in a huge arc
Step 7: Execute a 'loop-the-poop'[3], landing a big dollop of the brown stuff onto fast car (preferably a Ferrari, Lamborghini or Porsche.)
Step 8: Sit on the bonnet of the car to build up speed for the final move
Step 9: Soar over the bus from Step 1 into a quadruple-somersault quadruple-poo (READER WARNING: DO NOT TRY THIS AT HOME)
Step 10: Land on a traffic cone on one foot
Step 11: On top of the cone, finish with a ballet pirouette, and a backflip to land
Step 12: Mark the end of the routine with a tiny, delicate poop
Step 13: Bow to the crowd

It was an audacious plan, but where better to execute it than the Poopfest Games. MTM's legendary status would be confirmed or crushed, depending on the outcome.

When it finally came to competition day, thousands of birds from across the capital came to witness the spectacle. They all came to see MTM attempt 'The Death Wish'. Some of them actually wanted to see MTM get flattened - her critics said that she was over the hill, and due her comeuppance. But the majority were there to see art. Poetry in motion.

And at first, poetry is what they got. Matilda executed steps 1 through 10 with sheer perfection, even completing the never seen before quad-somersault quad-poo, which set a new world record for 'most acrobatic rotations with simultaneous defecation'. It was a glorious display. Not a toe out of place, not a single poop missed.

However, by Step 11, the landing, MTM was starting to feel tired, and the quadruple-somersault she had just done made her incredibly dizzy.

Gliding down towards the traffic cone for the final phase of the routine, she approached with one foot outstretched. As she landed on top of the cone, it wobbled to one side, and MTM lost her footing. She slipped, lost balance. In slow motion, she watched her fantasy of perfection disappear forever. While she knew now that the routine could never be considered flawless, she wanted to finish in style, like the true professional she was. She used her momentum from the slip to begin the ballet pirouette, and started spinning. In her original routine, she had only planned to do one pirouette turn, but because of her mistake, she wanted to compensate. She whizzed around, completing one, two, three, four, five turns, and kept going. She went from dizzy to downright delusional, and looked like she was going to pass out. After 18 spins, she had totally forgotten where she was.

MTM was hurtling out of control. Her feathers became so tucked in, she looked like a grey pencil caught in a tornado. She began to lose consciousness, and started to drop back down towards the open rim at the top of the traffic cone. She was going to fall into it!

---

[3] A loop-the-loop with a poop midway through the manoeuvre. Bonus points are awarded for landing the poop onto expensive cars, for the increased risk factor.

Her fans watched, beaks agape, and rushed to save her. Perhaps they could move the cone, or push her out of the way before she dropped in. By the time they reached her, it was already too late. Matilda had fallen in at the top of the cone, and was wedged in at the wings. She was trapped.

Paddy hurried over to the scene, along with a horde of birds that wanted to help. They had to get her off the road, before anything worse happened. They couldn't pull her out, so had to move the whole cone with MTM stuck inside. With a monumental effort, the crowd helped to lift the traffic cone off the ground and flew it back to the nest, all while Matilda was stuck at the top, her frazzled head poking above the rim.

Once they'd returned to the nest, Matilda began to recover her senses, but couldn't move. The fans tried everything to get her out. They pulled and pecked at the plastic cone for hours, desperately trying to set their hero free. When that didn't work, visiting birds began showering MTM with flowers and gifts, hoping that these would magically release her from her conical prison. It continued long into the night. The traffic cone became a sort of bizarre fluorescent shrine, and MTM was held aloft like a goddess.

It was no use, though, and the remaining fans returned home in the early hours.

The next morning, when it was just Paddy and his mum left, he asked:

'What are we going to do?'

'I'll have to go on a diet', Matilda replied. 'I ate too much pizza in training. It's made me fat. If I can shed some weight, I'll slip right down through this cone and break free'.

'How long will it take, Mum?'

'I don't know. Maybe a month, maybe more. Look, don't you worry about me Paddy. You've worried about me for far too long, and your father and I have been a terrible burden on you. I think now it is time that you start your own journey. Whatever that may be, wherever you may go, I think it is time that you became your own bird. By the time you come back, I will have lost enough weight that I'll be free again, and I *promise* that there will be no more stunts. Just make sure you don't forget to come home, like your sorry excuse for a father. Now go, before I start weeping and demanding that you stay. I love you, little chick'.

Paddy looked a mixture of confused and sad and worried all at the same time, and mumbled 'I love you too, Mum'. He was kind of terrified, but his mum was usually right – it was time for him to go. At least MTM was safe, wedged in tightly to her traffic cone in the nest.

So into the wide world Paddy went.

2

Young Paddy set out on the streets of London. He still couldn't quite believe what had happened to his mum, and how quickly he found himself alone. But he didn't dwell on it, because pigeons have a tendency to lose track of where they are and what they're doing. He came to thinking about his next move.

He instantly knew where to head: Trafalgar Square. He'd been told all his life that it was pigeon paradise: thousands upon thousands of birds to make friends with, many high ledges to perch on, and most importantly, lots of littering people leaving snacks behind.

Paddy's mum had never let him go before. She always said it was too dangerous, in spite of the fact that she was the world-famous daredevil MTM. It never seemed fair that she got to flip and spin her way in and out of trouble, while Paddy stayed rooted to the spot. Now, it was his mum who was well and truly stuck, and Paddy was free to go where he wanted, so long as he made it back home, eventually. In his mum's words, he had to 'become his own bird'. He wasn't really sure what that meant yet, but he assumed that he probably had to go out and do some stuff.

But how to get to Trafalgar? Paddy had been beyond his local borough before, but never alone. He knew he had to head south, towards central London, and ever so slightly east, towards Westminster, but that was about it. Luckily however, if there's one direction any bird knows, it's south.[4] From there, Paddy could work out east, using the 'Never Eat Shredded Wheat' method.

Getting out of his nesting area was the first task, and no mean feat at that. Paddy lived in a barmy place called Camden Town, which had already taken him a lifetime to learn to navigate.

Camden is a complete world within a city, a twisting labyrinth of backstreets, canals, bridges and tunnels; vibrant and bohemian, filled with all manner of brilliant people, mad as hatters, adorned with bells, whistles, chains, and famously, giant leather boots. Camden is *nearly* always busy, and *always* always bonkers. Paddy knew his way around, but there was no telling what would be in store for him on any given day.

---

[4] In case you didn't know, birds migrate seasonally. They often travel south during winter where more food will be available. Birds can do this without even thinking. It's second nature, like putting on your underpants. Neither birds nor humans can forget to do either of these tasks, or they'll be caught cold.

Paddy decided that he would need some fuel if he was going to weave his way through the chaos and reach the other side of town with all his toes intact. In fact, the street food at Camden Market would make a perfect breakfast. The previous night's leftovers always served up a special pick 'n' mix for a pigeon, which is otherwise known as '*fusion food*' in the bird world. At Camden Market in particular, there was often an unexpected surprise thrown in the mix, coughed up from the canal, or worse, the sewers.

Paddy's favourite was Asian cuisine – he especially loved Chinese, Lebanese, Burmese, Japanese, Taiwanese, Vietnamese - all the -eses together. He liked the way they rhymed.

Sometimes his flavour combinations tasted great:

Chicken masala with squashed banana
Pad Thai with crusty pie and even:
Canal maggots with muddy carrots[5]

But sometimes the combinations didn't work:

Bubble tea with toilet wee
Stir-fried noodles with hair of poodle
Avocado maki with baby's nappy and even:
Chunks of old boot with ginger root

Paddy's breakfast was more standard fare this time around: a half-English. Kind of like a full English, but with half the ingredients. Pigeons rarely get a full anything, so have to take what they can get. Fortunately for Paddy, on this day he had quite a haul. He scoured the Camden cobblestones and managed to find bits of discarded sausage, a few baked beans, trampled eggs (never fried), and some sort of potato thing, instead of a hash brown. He noticed that nobody ever drops their actual hash browns, probably because they taste so incredible, like hot, crispy clouds of potatoey goodness.

Paddy always dreamed of one day having the complete English breakfast, with tea and toast and all the trimmings (including black pudding, even though it's mostly blood and guts and disgusting wibbly bits).

Still, he was quite pleased with his share today, and was grateful just to have something resembling breakfast. So he ate, scrap upon scrap until he was full, and ate some more just to be sure.

A half-English always set him up well on difficult days, and didn't give him such a wobbly stomach, like when he had '*fusion food*'. He couldn't risk an explosive gut in such a bustling place as Camden, because something nasty might drop on a person's head

---

[5] Perhaps not the most appetising menu for the human palate. You'll have to trust me that for birds, these are glorious combinations.

or worse, in their food. He certainly didn't want to anger the local folk in the giant leather boots, who might have stamped on him if he pooped in the wrong place.

So, weighed down by his hearty meal, Paddy began to sluggishly duck and bob his way through the market, steering clear of the punks, hippies and other mysterious residents of Camden.

As he blended into the throng, he eased into his surroundings, soaking up the lively morning atmosphere. A delicious waft of freshly baked pastries crept up his nostrils. Street sellers called to one another in friendly voices. Upbeat music erupted from the street speakers. If birds could smile, Paddy would have done.

Yet not everyone at the market seemed as content as he felt inside. Paddy soon came across a tired-looking man with an unkempt beard and dark, lonely eyes. He looked terribly sad, sadder than the other Camden folk, that was for sure. In contrast to the surrounding miniature world of colour, this man was dull and drained. The man was sat with no shoes on, on a tattered piece of cardboard, holding a sign which said:

'Any kind gesture would be greatly appreciated. Thank you, Jim xx'

Paddy didn't really understand what this meant, so began lumbering past, minding his own business. He'd always been taught to avoid people who stood out, or looked unhappy and alone. It was safer, apparently. In spite of that, Paddy's instincts told him to help the man. He just wasn't sure how.

He had almost passed him, when he noticed a cup on the ground. It was in front of one of the man's grubby feet, and contained a few coins. An idea was coming to Paddy.

'He must be a *coin* collector!' Paddy whispered excitedly to himself, as he realised that not 2 minutes ago he'd seen a pound on the floor. He felt compelled to retrieve it to give the man something for his collection. Paddy retraced his steps.

Now that Paddy had started to digest his morning meal, he could actually get himself off the ground, so he flew to the coin and brought it back in no time at all. He dropped it in the cup, and the man's blue eyes lit up.

'For me?! Thank you, little birdy. Here, take these', the man said, and he offered some breadcrumbs from his pocket.

Paddy obliged, pecking the crumbs from the man's palm, and felt all fuzzy inside.

It was a genuine honour for Paddy to help a fellow collector, especially one who was barefoot and alone, just like him. He wondered what types of things he would collect for himself once arriving at Trafalgar Square: shiny foil, banknotes, souvenirs - perhaps things he'd never even dreamed of.[6]

With renewed excitement, Paddy set off again, working his way through Camden's crowds, taking special care to avoid the unpredictable dogs and deranged children that seemed to be pursuing him. Every time he dodged out of the way, there was a new threat. He couldn't even pause for a breath; it would only put him in more danger. He simply had to keep moving. So he went on, putting toe in front of toe, all the while escaping kicks, swipes, stomps, and flying objects.

Until suddenly, a little bit of peace. Paddy had, until then, been feeling as though he was caught in a whirlwind. Somehow, he'd been spewed out the other side, on the south side of Camden and entering St. Pancras. He was out of breath, and a tad dizzy, but otherwise alive. Trafalgar couldn't be far now, he thought. He decided he was never going to give up on his destination, even if he got distracted here and there. Getting distracted was part of being a pigeon, after all.

---

[6] It should be noted that pigeons are avid collectors. All birds love collecting twigs and leaves, of course, but pigeons have a special liking for rare titbits. So much so in fact, that each year a pigeon collectors' convention is held in Richmond park, where pigeons from all over the world bring their peculiar findings for comparison. Last year's claimant of the overall prize, Linti Harvesta of Spain, won for an outstanding collection of human belly button fluff. Unfortunately, her title was revoked after it was discovered that the 'fluff' was actually the mass of downy feathers shed by her 14 chicks, several years before.

3

As the rising sun warmed Paddy's tiny heart, another distraction came, in the form of an old looking church in St. Pancras, conveniently named: St. Pancras Old Church. It looked stark and beautiful against the pale winter sky. Going there would take him a little off course, but Paddy felt inexorably drawn to it, so went there anyway.

Following his instincts had worked for him in Camden. Surely they would set him right again.

Paddy loved old buildings too. They provided nooks and crannies for shelter, secret towers for storing food, and frankly, nobody seemed to care if he took humungous poos all over the rooves.

Paddy especially loved churches, for their graveyards. He enjoyed reading the headstones, to find out about what people of the past were like.[7] The graves gave Paddy a glimpse into the human world, enough for him to imagine entire lifetimes from hundreds of years ago. It was one of his favourite ways to pass the time.

He waddled over to the biggest tomb he could find at St. Pancras, and read the inscription:

Sir John Soane

Architect of the Bank of England

Who departed this life on 20th January 1837

Aged 84 years

'An architect – fascinating…' Paddy muttered to himself. 'From the 1800s too! I bet he designed loads of awesome buildings that are still standing today. It even says he worked on the Bank of England. *The Bank of bloomin' England*! The Bank…of… *England*…hang on - why is that familiar?'

---

[7] If you're questioning whether birds can read, think again. Paddy learned very easily, by staring at the daily newspapers over the shoulders of commuters. His favourite section was the obituaries, because he could find out about someone's whole life in just a few paragraphs. Naturally, Pigeons struggle to digest and retain more information than that. Still, there's a lot more knowledge crammed into those pea-sized brains than you might have thought possible.

Instead of picturing the wonderful life of this architect, as Paddy would have done normally, he began to feel his skin crawl with anxiety as he realised something terrible.

It dawned on Paddy that during his early years, he'd dropped thousands upon thousands of savage poo-bombs on the Bank of England, while on training excursions with his mum. This poor man, Sir John Soane, had dedicated his life to designing buildings, and all Paddy had done was relieve himself on them!

Sir John Soane was a knight too, which probably meant he could come back from the dead, carrying weapons and armour, riding a majestic phantom steed, ready to punish any one or thing that wronged him since his death. Paddy, on the other hand, was a defenceless little bird – what hope did he have against a vengeful ghost-knight? He immediately broke out into a cold sweat, worried that the architect's ghostly hands would rise out of his grave and wring Paddy's neck for his pooey crimes. Paddy gulped, twice, and cast sideways glances, to pretend he was looking anywhere but John Soane's grave.

But wherever he looked, he seemed to catch the eye of a crow. These birds are the spooky residents of cemeteries up and down the country, and this cemetery was no different. The crows were at least three times Paddy's size, and their ragged, jet black feathers made him shudder with fear. They cawed and squawked in grisly tones, as if to warn Paddy: 'Don't mess with Sir John Soane. He's resting in peace, and if you wake him up from his eternal sleep, he will *hunt* you down'.

The lead crow was larger than the rest: a raven. She was a magnificent, lustrous, stately-looking bird, who looked less than impressed at Paddy's presence in her graveyard. She began striding towards Paddy, swiftly followed by her sinister looking cronies.

Paddy turned his head over his wing, hoping that the crows were instead heading towards something behind him. No chance. As soon Paddy turned his head back, the beastly birds were upon him. Make no mistake, they were here for Paddy, and noone else. Nowhere to run, nowhere to hide. An army of crows came to loom over the quivering pigeon, and the imposing raven stood tall at the front, leading her troops. She pointed her knife-edged beak in Paddy's direction.

'My, my, my. Well aren't you a lost little lamb', the raven sneered.

'Uh…I am, a bit. I'm..I'm looking for Trafalgar Square. Would anyone in your g-group know how to get there?' Paddy asked. In truth, he didn't much care for directions right now. He was merely praying that the crows wouldn't ask him about Sir John Soane and the incidents at the Bank of England.

The raven replied: 'Anyone in our "group", you ask. I'm afraid you're very much mistaken'.

'Oh…' Paddy mumbled.

The raven took on the tone of a disappointed headmistress: 'Very…much…mistaken. We're no group, but a MURDER. A MURDER of crows'.

'A… a murder?' Paddy asked nervously.

'Pff- pigeons really are as dim-witted as they look, aren't they'. The other crows were sniggering, as the raven went on: 'Allow me to enlighten you and that miniscule brain of yours: a 'murder' is our collective noun, the unique title for all us crows together. You might have heard of a "wisdom…of owls", a "squabble…of seagulls", or, for a collection of your scrawny bunch: a "loft…of pigeons"'.' We crows spend a great deal of time dealing with murder, so murder is our name. You see, we are undertakers, or supreme guardians of the dead, if you prefer'.

'Guardians… of the dead?' Paddy became ice-cold with fear. He was certain at this point that he wasn't far away from being murdered himself.

'That's right, young squire. Once birds have popped their clogs, we collect the bodies and bones, the feathers and feet, the beaks and the wings and all the wibbly bits inbetween'. The raven's expression contorted into a twisted smile. Then she ran her tongue around the rim of her beak, as if she were about to feast on all the decaying birdy parts she had just described. 'We crows hold the keys to the afterlife, and we'll have to decide whether we let you through one day. Only if we like you, of course.'

The crows' ominous laughter rumbled through the graveyard. Paddy felt rather unsettled, and was starting to feel his belly turn over. He definitely wasn't planning on visiting the afterlife any time soon.

The raven seemed to have little else to say, but her companions wanted a piece of the action. These birds looked almost a different species compared to their regal and aloof leader. They were hardy birds; battered and bruised, with mischievous glints in their eyes. They shuffled from side to side, as if ready for a fight. One of them piped up, in a rasping cockney accent:

'All the birds round 'ere come to us once they've died, and we do *all* the dirty work getting 'em 'ere. You wouldn't wanna know 'alf the things I've seen, little pidge. Worse than your nightmares, believe me'.

The crows' laughter grew to a bellowing cackle. Paddy was trembling, and slyly trying to shuffle his way out of this situation. The crows were toying with him. Paddy motioned to leave, but was stopped in his tracks by the raven.

'Hold it right there', she ordered Paddy. 'Your face is familiar. What's your name?'

'Erm - Patrick Jr. R02390'

'Patrick Jr. R02390? Son of Patrick Sr. R02390? Grandson of Patrick the poet? And Great Grandson of Pat the pot?'

The "guardians of the dead" were shrieking with excitement at this possible revelation. Paddy couldn't back out now.

'Yes - that's me, I think,' Paddy said hesitantly. 'But I haven't seen my Dad in years, and I never met my Granddad. As for Pat the pot – I've got no idea what you're talking about. Look, I should be er…moving on'.

There was another pause. A hollow stillness. The laughter stopped. Paddy sensed trouble. Had he offended the crows? They started to look threatening again, as if they might be taking him to the afterlife, straight away. Then, all the crows simultaneously bowed towards Paddy, as though they might attack. The raven also bowed. Paddy shut his eyes, in anticipation of his own death, until the raven said:

'It is a tremendous privilege to welcome you to our graveyard, Patrick, son of Patrick, grandson of Patrick, great grandson of Patrick. I am the Morrigan, queen of crows, and gatekeeper to the avian afterworld. The folks behind me are my comrades.'

'Oh..It's a… privilege to meet you all too', Paddy replied hesitantly, still wincing with one eye closed, anticipating pain. 'But I'm not ready to die just yet'.

The crows resumed their raucous cackling. This was all side-splittingly funny for them. One crow was even slapping her knee with her wing.[8] Paddy, meanwhile, didn't know whether to laugh or cry. He was utterly dumfounded.

'Allow me to explain', the Morrigan said, softening her tone. 'We're not taking you to the world of the dead just yet. It's true that everyone must go there eventually, and it *is* my job to send birds on their merry way to the afterlife, but you're still a young pidge, about to make your mark on the world. We've been pulling your leg the whole time. I must confess, we get quite a kick out of tormenting our guests, but I'm afraid the joke's been lost on you. It's nothing personal. Please accept my humble apologies - we crows don't get out much. I'd hate to start on bad terms with the fourth Patrick in the line of Patricks'.

The crows bowed for a second time, this time more elaborately, to make the point clear.

---

[8] Birds do in fact have knees, in case you were wondering. Contrary to popular belief, they bend the same way as human knees, but they are concealed by feathers, high up on the leg, so nobody gets to see them. The funny bit that bends backwards on a bird leg - the bit that look like a backwards knee - That's more like a human ankle, if anything. Trust me, I'm an ornithologist. Well, not really, but it sounds good.

'Well, apology accepted', Paddy said, scratching his head, 'but I don't think your jokes are very funny'. He bowed in response, still with some trepidation. 'How do you know about my family? And who was Pat the pot?'

The cockney crow interjected again: 'We know *all* about yer family 'istory, Patrick Jr. We know the 'istories of every bird from 'ere to 'ighgate. As undertakers, we get to see all the birds from this area, eventually. I'll admit, they're not in the best shape when we meet 'em!' The other crows squawked in agreement. 'Don't worry yourself though young Patrick, you come from fine stock indeed: artists, athletes, and alcoholics alike!'

'Alcoholics?! Was that my great-granddad then?'

The crows were now hysterical. In their eyes, if a topic was morbid, macabre or depressing, it was funny. It was the blackest of black comedy.

The Morrigan showed some sympathy for Paddy, and calmed her followers down, before adding: 'Oh yes, young squire. Pat the pot was a flat-out drunk. He used to perch in pub gardens, waiting for people to leave their pints, so he could swoop in and guzzle down the beer while nobody was looking. He was a real sneak! The loopiest in the land. In fact, if birds had an Olympic drinking team, he would be the coach.' All the undertakers guffawed and beat their wings with laughter.

'Oh, right, well thanks for telling me, I guess'. Paddy said, confusedly. 'Why is it you all laugh so much if you're around the dead all the time?'

'If you don't laugh, young Patrick, you'll cry,' the Morrigan said.

'I suppose you're right', Paddy agreed meekly. He didn't look convinced.

'What a sober young fellow', another of the crows said, turning to his friends, tilting his head in Paddy's direction. 'I know what *he* needs – a good drink!'

Paddy had to smile, because he couldn't think of anything else to do, around these jokers.

The cockney chimed in once more: 'Don't drink too much though, or you might be meeting us in the afterlife sooner than you'd like!'

The Morrigan settled the crows again, and returned her attention to Patrick's original request:

'Look Patrick, you could do with some work on your sense of humour, but since your Great-Grandfather provided us with plenty of laughs, we'll help you out.

Firstly, a gift from me. I, as the birdy goddess of the afterlife, have certain special powers that I can grant to deserving birds. These powers either have the capability to help someone conquer their greatest battles, or may do the opposite, and condemn them to a fate of doom. I confer my powers based on whether a bird has lived a life of love and compassion, or of greed and cruelty.

Paddy was once again terrified, silently pleading he'd be granted the all-conquering powers instead of the fate of doom. He liked to think that he was, for the most part at least, loving and compassionate'.

The Morrigan continued: 'I noticed, for instance that you recently helped a lonely barefooted man in Camden'.

'You saw that?' Paddy responded incredulously. He shuddered. The Morrigan had been watching him.

'Indeed – I have eyes, ears and beaks everywhere, and for this display of compassion and generosity, I will bestow to you the powers of almighty courage, for I suspect that you will need it on your journey ahead. It will aid you in times of great need.'

What a relief. The Morrigan had found favour in the young bird. Paddy mopped his brow, thankful that he wouldn't be headed for doom, any time soon.

'How will I get the powers of courage to work, or when to use them?' he asked.

'You must listen to your heart and soul, when your head tells you that something is impossible'.

This made no sense whatsoever to Paddy. It seemed that the Morrigan was speaking in a secret code language, which only goddesses and gods could understand. He was trying to work out how exactly one listens to their heart, but was too intimidated to ask any more questions.

'Take heed though, young Patrick'. The Morrigan warned. 'If you forsake your *heart and soul*, in exchange for despair, suspicion and anger, I will be taking your heart and soul for myself. Birds that fail to use these faculties, clearly don't have a need for them, so I like to borrow them from time to time and put them to better use, in the afterworld. As I'm sure you'll understand, the world of the dead could always do with a little extra heart and soul. Make sure you use yours, or I may be paying you an unwanted visit'.

As for your directions to Trafalgar, unfortunately my awareness of London extends only as far as the spirit world, so I will defer to the rest of the murder, who know the streets round here far better than I. I hope you'll get to Trafalgar in one piece. Nice meeting you, young Patrick, and I'll see you in the afterlife, sometime.'

Before Paddy could speak again, The Morrigan's body dissolved into a black, misty vapour, and she was gone. The mist settled on the grass, and merged with the morning dew. Paddy felt a chill down his spine. He was speechless. He had hundreds of questions racing through his mind:

'Did The Morrigan really hold the keys to the afterlife? What did that even mean? Why was she here? Was she even here at all? How am I still alive? What was all that about heart and soul? Am I going crazy?'

Gradually, the noise of bickering crows rose up above the questioning noises in his head.

'I know London like the back of my talon', an old crow, with greying, faded feathers, called out.

'No you don't, you old fool!' a young upstart responded. 'Only birds of prey have talons. What you mean to say is, I know London like the back of my feet.'

'Well you all bleedin' know what I mean'. The old crow snapped back. 'I've been roaming the London streets and skies for nigh on 30 years now. 30 years! That's more than all of you combined.' The young crows rolled their eyes, and made mocking snoozing sounds, as if to say they'd heard the old crow's spiel many times before.

'Ignore them, young Patrick', the old crow said. 'All you need to do is go directly south from here, 1.9 miles, as the crow flies. You might be a fraction of a degree to the west, but you should see Lord Nelson peeping above the rooftops. When you get to him, you'll be right in the middle of Trafalgar Square. You'll find him easy. He's only got one arm, so leans on his sword for balance. He's always wearing a wide brimmed hat, too. All these years I've been going down there, and he hasn't moved an inch, and he's *never* changed his clothes'.

'That's cause he's a statue, you old git!' The young crows were now shaking their heads with despair. 'Ignore the old timer, Paddy, the tube's where it's at these days. You'll be in Trafalgar in 10 minutes flat. The old git may have been doing that journey for 30 years, but flying? *So* slow, and boring as hell. We all do that every day. The tube is *way* more exciting. Here's what you need to do: head down Pancras Road, which merges into Midland Road, go past the big red Renaissance Hotel, turn left into King's Cross station, down the stairs, over the barrier, down the escalator, through the tunnel. Get on the train, two stops on the Victoria line down to Oxford Circus, southbound towards Brixton. Change platforms. Get on a Bakerloo line train for another two stops, southbound, this time towards Elephant & Castle, and get off at Charing Cross. Up the stairs, through the tunnel, up the escalator, over the barriers, into the daylight, and voilà – Trafalgar Square'.

'The other directions seem much less confusing to me', Paddy said.

'Ah, it's a piece of cake, don't worry. Just remember, Kings Cross to Charing Cross, and voila!'

'Well, when you say it like that it sounds easy'.

'It is! Trust us. The only way to explore is to do what hasn't been done before. Besides, you'll get there in half the time. Ask yourself this question: do you want to be a daring young bird? Or a miserable old git, knocking at death's door?'

Paddy acquiesced. Flying seemed like the easy option, but he didn't want to be a miserable old git, not least when the gatekeeper of the afterlife had just paid him a visit. The tube was starting to make sense, he decided.

'King's Cross to Charing Cross, and voila!' the young upstart repeated. 'Good luck, Patrick son of Patricks'.

Paddy thanked the young crows, and made leave for the underground.

The undertakers split off, with parting shrieks of laughter.

All except the old crow, who was fuming.

4

King's Cross station was only a short distance from the church, so Paddy got swiftly back on track, in his pursuit of pigeon paradise.

He had left the graveyard a little bit spooked. Paddy wasn't sure if the crows from the church had been malicious, or strangely charming? He couldn't tell. They sure joked a lot. But was it at Paddy's expense? And the way the Morrigan disappeared – it must have been some sort of dark magic. It was terrifying, but thrilling at the same time. He couldn't wait to tell his Mum what he'd seen.

Not, of course, before visiting the famous Trafalgar Square. All he had to remember was King's Cross to Charing Cross, and Voila!

Paddy knew it'd be safer to fly there, as per the old crow's instructions. But Paddy's Mum was so daring in her job, why couldn't he be too? He simply had to take the tube, to prove something to himself more than anything.

Paddy headed back out through the church gates, and trotted on down Midland Road towards the station, carefully sticking to the pavement. Flying up onto a street lamp for a better vantage point, he was able to see the grand red brick exterior of the Renaissance hotel, as described by the crows. Thankfully, he was going in the right direction.

And once he got closer, he saw signs for the train station.

This really was proving to be as straightforward as the young crows suggested. Paddy felt a surge of confidence as he saw several underground signs in the famous red and blue signage. He no longer felt like the lowly bird he looked.

So, at that point, he pretended he was a majestic golden eagle, soaring over the tip of the London skyline. In one swoop, he glided the final 50 metres to one of the station entrances. Then, he tottered inside.

Upon entering, Paddy was awestruck by the cavernous glass rooves and towering windows. It was staggering.[9] The huge clock high up on the rear wall read 10 thirty. It was a giant reminder that he had plenty of time to get to Trafalgar and home before the end of the day. He was brimming with optimism.

Until he got lost.

---

[9] Remember that a pigeon, 50 times shorter than your average human, sees things 50 times larger.

During Paddy's brief eagle-soar, he'd noticed a number of entrances. But which entrance corresponded to which station? There were at least 3 King's Cross Stations close by. He had just tried the closest one. He *assumed* any entrance would be good.

The fear began to set back in.

Waddling about, searching for the Victoria line entrance, Paddy was sucked into the enormity of King's Cross station. The interior of the building seemed to be endlessly expanding above him, and the glass shapes of the walls and ceilings appeared to swivel and interlock, like a kaleidoscope. He was stuck inside a moving puzzle, a Rubik's cube of epic proportions.

Paddy's mind wandered. He resorted to pecking up flaky bits of croissant, before being drawn to a bizarre luggage trolley half-stuck into the wall. Luggage trolleys were designed to be moved around, he thought. This one was wedged into the brickwork! He'd never seen anything like it. And it had a platform number above. 9¾. How strange. All the other platform numbers were whole numbers. Maybe this train only took you ¾ of the way there.

He suspected it wouldn't be the right train to anywhere, but he temporarily felt safe here, like it would be a good place to get his bearings.

On top of the trolley, there was a white owl in a cage, so Paddy thought that birds would be welcome. Not long after he had perched though, a little boy came over and shooed him away, shouting: 'go away pidgy, I just want a photo with Hedwig, not you'.

Paddy didn't really understand human-speak, but he was used to being made subordinate to birds of prey. Owls were higher up the food chain, after all. Paddy narrowly avoided the child's swiping hand, and scurried off into the station concourse. He kept his head down and kept moving, hoping that the Victoria line would magically reveal itself to him. Maybe the Morrigan's powers of courage would show him the way.

He couldn't see a sign for Charing Cross. Nor for the Victoria line, or the Bakerloo. Nothing even for the tube now. Instead, just names for destinations he'd never heard of: Gare du Nord, Lyon, Brussels.

Out of nowhere, he arrived at the foot of a huge blue billboard. It read: 'A short hop from King's Cross, and voila!' Paddy couldn't believe his luck. He said to himself: 'It's just like the crows said: King's Cross to Charing Cross, and voila! This must be the direct train to Charing Cross!'

He walked beneath the sign and found himself at the back of a long human queue. He was convinced this was the queue for paradise. Unfortunately, waiting in line would mean that people and bags would tower above him. It was agitating for Paddy, to say the least.

The advantage of being a pigeon is that one doesn't have to wait in line. Paddy soared over the crowds of people, and instantly felt calmer. He came to perch on one of the station's steel roof beams, high up above the queue, for a bird's eye view.

He looked down. A meandering stream of people were being funnelled into the train. Paddy decided he would wait, until the very last person boarded. He couldn't be seen by the guards, of course.

Trafalgar was a popular destination, but Paddy couldn't help but ask himself: was it possible that this many people were going there? And what were they doing with all their bags?

A few minutes passed, and now Paddy was starting to question the young crows who told him to take the train. They said he'd be there in 10 minutes flat. It'd been 10 minutes already!

Paddy held his nerve a little longer, as the people below continued boarding.

As the final person set foot on the train, Paddy shut out the doubts in his head, and swept down to the platform.

Being in a hurry, his landing was clumsy. Somewhat less graceful than his eagle-esque approach of before. But that didn't matter now.

Paddy stared up at the giant open train doorway ahead of him. Everybody was seated, and the guards had their backs turned. This was his moment.

Paddy puffed his chest up, and said to himself, 'become your own bird!'.

Without thinking, he hopped up onto the ledge, and shuffled his way in. He couldn't believe his own bravery. Were the Morrigan's powers of courage guiding him? Quite possibly.

Paddy was standing, alone, between two cabins, which were filled with people. Luckily, there were doors between him and the cabins, which had closed, so shut him off from view of the passengers.

There was some luggage stacked in the corner. Paddy took cover behind it, and positioned himself neatly between a bag and the wall behind him, so nobody would have any idea he was there.

Paddy exhaled with a sigh, and closed his eyes. He was in.

He was perfectly concealed. All he had to do was keep his eyes closed, for probably less than 10 minutes, and he'd be in Trafalgar.

The doors closed and locked with an irrevocable clench. Some undecipherable human-speak came out from the speaker system.

Excitement bubbled up from the pit of Paddy's stomach, and exploded through his entire body. Paradise was close.

As long as he stayed calm, he'd be fine. He was out of sight, out of mind.

Unfortunately, pigeons being restless creatures, he couldn't stay still for long.

Paddy remained mostly hidden, but popped his head up above the suitcase that was giving him cover. In typical bird fashion, he jerked his head left and right, eagerly looking for something shiny or attention grabbing.

The only thing that looked remotely interesting was a poster, stuck to one of the inside walls of the train. It looked remarkably similar to the billboard he'd seen in the station. However, it contained some extra information.

It read:

Welcome aboard this Eurostar train. A short hop from King's Cross, and voila! You're in Paris - Gare du Nord. Journey time is approximately 2 hours and 16 minutes. Refreshments will be available to purchase from the onboard trolley. We hope you enjoy your journey to the city of love.

Paddy's eyes popped.

'Eurostar? 2 hours and 16 minutes?! Paris!' He said to himself breathlessly.

Paddy instinctively stumbled out of his hiding place and toppled onto the floor. In a blistering panic, he threw himself, with all his might, into the train's full-length glass doors that had just closed behind him, hoping he would fly straight through them and back into the open air.

With a dull thud, he bounced right off the glass, and grimaced, as he landed on his backside. He was sat with his legs splaying outwards, the way a toddler does after she's attempted to stand, and fallen backwards.

Paddy looked up at the window, oceans of tears cascading from his eyes.

Slowly at first, the train heaved itself forwards, pulling away from King's Cross, from London, from home.

5

What…a disaster.

Still drying his eyes, Paddy went through a continuous cycle of horror, fear, and panic.

He was stock-still, beak wide open, staring out of the full-length window ahead of him. The train picked up speed, and London's landscape melted into a furious concrete blur.

Once Paddy regained his senses, he retreated despondently to his previous hideout, behind the luggage in the corner. He was in between two sealed-off cabins, so he was safely out of sight of the passengers, for now. He kept as still as he could, but couldn't resist the odd jerky head movement or shake of his feathers. Luckily, nobody was around when he did so.

Paddy was questioning what had happened. Where had his wires been crossed? Why was he going to Paris and not Trafalgar? He thought it had been going so well, and that all he had to remember was King's Cross to Charing Cross, and voila!

To find out where he'd gone wrong, he popped his head up from behind the suitcase, for another read of the train's poster: A short hop from King's Cross, and voila!

It immediately clicked.

There was no mention of Charing Cross there, whatsoever. In his blind rushing, Paddy had ignored a crucial part of his journey. The destination!

He cursed his stupidity and naivety in trusting the young crows with their directions. He should have flown directly to Nelson and his column, just as the old crow had told him to. Paddy vowed that he would never again mistrust a wise head with 30 years experience, even if he was a grumpy old fogey.

Paddy had to collect himself.

'Paris isn't that far', he thought. After all, it could have been worse, *much* worse. He could have been trapped on a plane to the other side of the world. All Paddy would have to do, in theory, is hop off the train in Paris, change platforms, and get back on another Eurostar train to London. For now, that was the least of his worries. More pressing matters were at hand.

"First thing's first - refreshment", Paddy said under his breath.

He needed to find that snack trolley; the one mentioned on the poster. But he couldn't just march down the train to look for it. There'd be a riot! Paddy needed to put in place a food strategy. 2 hours without a snack for a pigeon is entirely intolerable. In the open air, it's no problem. Fly to a different spot, find a new snack. Run out of snacks, go somewhere else. But in a crowded train, he would need to be stealthy. Pigeons aren't expected, nor desired, in such places.

Minutes later, a miraculous opportunity arose. A hissing, whooshing sound of air burst out. It sounded like the airlock release of a spacecraft. One of the cabin doors was sliding open.

A snack trolley, filled with treats, gradually emerged through the sliding door from the cabin to his right, being carefully pushed and pulled by two of the train's staff members.

Paddy kept himself concealed behind the bags, but could just about make out the tops of people's heads as the cabin door had opened. Thankfully, none of the heads were looking his way.

As the food moved into his field of view, Paddy's eyes widened.

It looked, to him at least, as if an alien spaceship had just entered his domain, carrying all of his favourite snacks: salt & vinegar crisps, milk chocolate, and biscotti. Paddy was salivating.

Then, out of nowhere, a piercing cry rang out from the cabin where the trolley had just been.

Paddy noticed that the staff looked panicked. He couldn't understand what they were panicked about, but he could read their expressions. Had someone seen the pigeon hiding in the bags? Maybe the staff were discussing what to do.

Paddy instantly ducked for cover, to ensure he was out of view. Yet before long, the temptation to look at the snacks became too much for the young pigeon to bear. When he couldn't wait any longer, he cautiously peered over the top of the bags for another look at the snack trolley.

Astonishingly, the staff had disappeared. Paddy became convinced they'd gone to get help, and would return to come and capture Paddy, to eradicate the pigeon problem that was on board.

Paddy's gut feeling said he needed to move, to find a new hiding place.

Conveniently, the bottom shelf of the snack trolley was open and there was a perfectly pigeon-sized spot for Paddy to jump into. There were some crisppackets too, to shield him. What's more, Paddy could see a few tantalising crumbs scattered next to one of the wheels.

He eventually succumbed to the magnetising force of the scraps on the floor, and clambered out from behind the luggage, to peck away. If anybody came through the doors now, he'd be in full sight of not only the staff, but the passengers in the adjacent cabin.

Despite this, he pecked…and pecked…and pecked.

'Mmm, so salty, and vinegary', he said in his head. The tang was delightful.

After a period of intense gorging, Paddy snapped back to reality. He was fully exposed. The staff would be coming back soon, and if they hadn't seen him already, they'd almost certainly see him in the luggage area, which was now covered with loose pigeon feathers. The last thing he wanted, was to cause a scene.

Hoovering up the remaining scraps, Paddy hopped up onto the bottom shelf of the trolley, and nestled between some bags of crisps, for some protection from the outside world. In spite of that though, if anyone looked hard enough at the lower half of the trolley, Paddy would be seen, but it was unlikely, since people on trains are usually more concerned with looking out of the window, or stuffing food in their mouths, than what might be lurking in the bottom of the snack trolley. Paddy fancied his chances. After a brief crisp foil rustling when he had bundled his way in, all went quiet. The only remaining sound was the persistent rumbling of the train over the tracks.

Paddy had first satisfied his hunger, and now he felt safe and secure. All a bird needs, really. It was dark in the bottom shelf of the trolley, which was good. Easier to see out, than in. And the first thing Paddy saw, were two pairs of shiny black shoes re-positioning themselves at either ends of the trolley. The staff were back, unaware of the bird that was hidden beneath the snacks. Soon, they'd be moving on.

From Paddy's tucked away position, beneath a bag of McCoys Thai Sweet Chicken, he could hear muffled, indistinguishable voices above him. Was he being talked about? He certainly hoped not.

Then, the ground shifted. He felt himself moving on the trolley. The staff were pushing on to the next cabin. Paddy was effectively on a train *within* a train. His pulse jumped up a notch, or ten, as they entered the next cabin.

Surprisingly, the background noise shifted, somewhat agreeably to Paddy. It was more subdued, more refined in this part of the train. Paddy had no idea why, but the carpet had switched from a browny orange to a luxurious royal blue. He adjusted his view from within the trolley, between a bag of peanuts and a pack of crackers, to offer a better look. The royal blue carpet was soft, deep pile, with an elegant design. It looked sophisticated. Little did Paddy know, he had just entered first-class.

From Paddy's low position, he noticed other things too. Feet shuffling under seats, or tapping rhythmically. He even caught the eye of a small child who was crawling around on the floor and under the seats. Paddy expected a wail, a cry of terror from the youngster, at the sight of a bird on a train. Yet to this child, this situation was no more abnormal than what was already happening; being on a train that was going under the ocean to another country was crazy enough, probably. What difference did Paddy's presence make to her? She must have assumed it was all part of the experience. Entertainment for the journey.

She smiled and waved a little paw at Paddy. Paddy smiled in return.

The moment of connection between bird and baby was broken, by an outburst of smug, cackling laughter ringing throughout the cabin - the sound of money, to the human ear. Yet to Paddy, each laugh reminded him of the graveyard, and the screeching death-cries of the crows. If Paddy didn't survive this journey, the Morrigan and her cronies would most likely be coming for him: the undertakers preparing him for his afterlife.

One thing was for certain, and that was that Paddy would have loved to have used his powers of courage, to find a way out of this mess. Ironically, he was far too scared for that, so stayed right where he was.

His fear was amplified shortly afterwards. A staff member reached down to the lower part of the trolley for a bag of crisps, inches from where Paddy was laying. It was the only cover between him and the outside world of the cabin. If the staff member reached down for another bag of crisps, she would fumble for a packet, and instead grab a London street pigeon. Paddy needed a new hiding place. He needed to get off the train within the train.

He kept still while it moved on a few feet, before it pulled up beside an open weekend bag laying on the floor. The zips were open, and the bag revealed it's interior, invitingly for a pigeon looking for cover. It was comfortably large enough for Paddy to fit in, and would provide protection on all sides. In addition, the bag was finely crafted. Designer. Golden hand-stitching and a paisley silk lining. Yet Paddy didn't have a discerning eye for accessories. It may have been a designer bag for a person, but a designer bed, for a pigeon. It looked perfect.

In a moment of madness, Paddy hopped down onto the carpet. If the trolley moved now he'd be revealed to whole cabin. He had seconds to hop into the bag unseen. He wedged one leg in. Then the other. Followed by his head, and his right wing. The other, the left one…caught! Stuck in the zip. Paddy flapped hard, just once, out of sheer panic. He was freed, and in the bag. Some passengers sensed a disturbance, but the feeling soon passed away. The trolley moved on. That was close.

Paddy looked out from within, through the eye-shaped opening of the bag and onto the carpet. He could see feet shifting, stretching, resting. Paddy's heart slammed, almost ready to burst through his breast. How on earth would he get out of this?

After a few minutes of getting comfortable, inside the weekend bag, Paddy wrested back control of his senses. His pounding heart soon soothed and settled, as he nestled into the beautifully soft fabric. The bag was the warmest and cosiest nest he'd ever been in. He basked in its smoothness, and his worries, one by one, faded away.

His eyes slid shut. Paddy began to dream. He found himself in Trafalgar Square. Pigeon paradise. But it was empty. No people. No pigeons. Just Nelson, on top of his column. Then, Paddy saw something. A flash, a sparkle, a glimmer in Nelson's eye. Paddy was drawn to it, and soared upwards to inspect. The light was shiny and alluring and was getting brighter and bigger, and brighter and bigger still. It was the light at the end of the tunnel. Like being carried up to the heavens by angels. Paddy arrived in front of Nelson's body, floating, bathed in sunlight and warmth. Drifting on air. Magically, Nelson came to life. A moving stone statue. It was mesmerising. Nelson's first movement was to raise his sword with his one good hand. Paddy felt sure he was about to be knighted, and leaned forward, expecting the flat side of the blade to gently come down to his shoulder. Sir Patrick Jr. had a nice ring to it, he was thinking.

But no.

Instead, a vague, high-pitched squeal crescendoed, the kind of sound that might signal the end of the world, and rather than placing his sword on Paddy's shoulder, the moving statue swung for Paddy's neck. Paddy froze, hovering in the air at the height of Nelson's waist. The perfect height for a decapitation. Nelson swivelled, heaving his enormous stone sword towards Paddy's head. Paddy realised he could do nothing. Right as the fatal blow was delivered, and just as the sword struck, Paddy's eyes opened.

He had awoken from his dream to the nightmare of his reality.

'AHHHHHHHHHHHHHHH'. Shouts and yells were coming from all corners of the cabin.

Paddy's rise to Nelson in his dream was actually, in real life, the sensation of being lifted up while laying asleep in a designer bag. And the sound that sounded like the end of the world? That was the screeching of the bag's owner.

'It's a bird! A bloody bird in my bloody bag! Get it out. Out!'

Paddy did an involuntary poop, all over the bag's inner lining.

After a few seconds of being frozen-still, all hell broke loose. Paddy hurled himself upwards and out of the bag, straight into the ceiling of the train. With a big bump of his head, he spun around in a dizzy frenzy, desperately throwing himself into the windows to try and find fresh air.

Then another cry from the bag's owner, once they had *fully* inspected Paddy's makeshift nest:

'And he pooped in it too! I want him shot, put down, thrown in a cage. Punish the beast!'

There was pandemonium in the first class cabin. Umbrellas were opened to protect against any further poops, parents screamed and children mostly giggled, but most importantly for the passengers, all the other designer bags on board were rapidly zipped up and stowed away.

The staff members who had been pushing Paddy within the trolley, reached for a nearby bin. It was full with passenger rubbish, but this was an emergency. They emptied the contents of the bin into another bin, and the contents of that bin, into another one. Now, there were two empty bins. Two bird traps.

And brandishing the bin-traps, the staff squatted down like tennis players waiting to receive a serve, shifting their weight from foot to foot. They closed in, while the raucous, barely human noises provided the musical backdrop.

The first staff member made an impulsive dive for Paddy. The bin slammed onto the floor of the train.

Missed.

Paddy shuddered and instinctively bolted for the cabin exit. However, the doors were firmly shut, and securely, like the spacecraft airlock he'd imagined earlier. No getting out now. Paddy slammed and slammed, but as he lost energy, he could no longer resist the inevitability of capture.

As he fell for the final time, he felt his fall to the luxurious royal blue carpet in slow motion.

One of the black bins descended over Paddy's fragile and bruised frame. Its shadow was enveloping him. The Morrigan would surely be coming for him now, taking him to his birdy death. He had accepted his fate.

Paddy's world went black.

6

Darkness. Utter darkness. He was standing in a profound emptiness, which echoed with gloomy reverberations from beyond. Was this the afterworld? And could it have been, just possibly, that those distant sounds were the melancholy death-cries of the Morrigan?

Then, almost imperceptibly, a wide and narrow band of light appeared at his feet. It gradually broadened and heightened, until the darkness was fully replaced by light and colour and life. It was as if Paddy had been reborn into a brave new world.

And squinting into the harsh brightness, he realised that this was, in fact, not the world of the dead, but the world of the living.

The pigeon trap had been lifted.

Paddy turned, and found himself staring up at his captor: the lady among the train's staff who had covered him with the bin. She was ushering him off the now empty train, and onto the platform. Paddy shuffled forwards uncertainly, like a jar-trapped insect that doesn't know what do when it's been freed.

He noticed that the air smelled a little different now, but that the glass and steel surrounding him was much the same as in Kings Cross. The many concrete platforms and domed ceilings were not unlike the imposing architectures of home. Had Paddy even gone anywhere at all? He wasn't exactly sure.

Bearings needed to be gotten. And right on cue, there was another billboard to read:

Bienvenue à Paris

Welcome to Paris

Somehow, the journey, up to this point, had felt all too unreal. It wasn't until Paddy read the sign that he finally believed where he was.

Thankfully, he was alive, free, and uncaptured, which wasn't a bad start, in bird terms. But he was also lost, alone and tremendously afraid. Those were the things he would have to try and sort out.

He was also exhausted, and desperate for air. The prospect of a Eurostar journey back home was too petrifying to contemplate right now. He needed to get out of here, if only briefly, to merely breathe and collect his thoughts.

Following the train's now departed passengers, Paddy ensured that he kept his distance from any designer bags. After the chaotic events that occurred in the first-class cabin, the passengers were eager to leave the station quickly. Paddy's best route out would be to tail them from afar.

Up ahead, Paddy recognised the little girl from the train who had waved at him from under her seat. She was the only traveller on board who had showed him any kindness. Everybody else was calling for his head, *wanting* him dead.

The little girl was holding hands with her mum and dad. They were playing a game. As the young daughter held on tightly to the palms of her parents, she was lifted up and swung forwards several paces at once. This meant she could take colossal strides, like those of a giant. It looked fun.

The young girl was wearing a red and white polka dot dress, which meant that Paddy now had a brightly coloured object of focus that hopefully, would lead him right out and onto the street. The girl and her family appeared to be heading for the exit.

Paddy followed the red and white polka dots through tunnels, up escalators, and between barriers, all while maintaining the distance of a spy in silent pursuit.

As the polka dot dress finally showed him the way out of the station's entrance, Paddy was relieved that his plan had worked, for once.

At last, he stumbled out of Gare du Nord station, a sweaty and stinky bundle of feathers. Immediately, he noticed that he wasn't alone. There were pigeons *everywhere*. Scavengers of the skies, who had descended to greet the train travellers, and hoover up their mess.

A large crowd of birds were positioned close by, listening intently to a single lady pigeon[10], who stood on a raised podium above some steps. She was flamboyantly moving her wings and feet around in a strange kind of dance. But there was no music, no rhythm, just swift and chaotic movement. At least thirty birds were gathered, watching her at work.

What was it that she was doing?

Paddy edged closer, out of curiosity, and in need of friends in this foreign land. He began to make out some food scraps on the ground, which were being used as props in this

---

[10] A regular lady this time, not like the sycophantic lady pigeons who spent time with Paddy's famous dad.

lady's dance. In fact, it looked to him as though this bird was about to give some sort of lesson. That was it! She was going to cook. A pigeon chef, of all things. Un-believable.

'Now this delectable dish is my take on a Coq au Vin, pigeon style', she called out. 'If you don't know what that is, don't worry, I'm about to explain it to you. First, get yourself a discarded lighter. There's plenty of people smoking in this part of town so you'll find one of those easy. Then, set light to a crisp packet, and that's your spark. Get some twigs, and hold them to the flames. This is your stove'. As she demonstrated, a crackle of fire popped, making the pigeons in the front row flinch and back up a few feet. No bird wants a singed eyebrow or a burnt feather.[11]

The chef described the next steps:

'Start with half-eaten chicken bones, and some of Saturday night's spilled wine: that's your base. Put the chicken with the wine, they have a good time, I say. Anything you can add on top is a bonus. Pork scratchings serve well instead of lardons (there aren't many of those just lying about, you know!). Add some mushrooms, if you're lucky, and a bit of moss mixed with mud for nutrition – it all works *wonders* for your skin'. The chef finished her demonstration with a flourish, before saying: and there you have it. Voila!'

That word made Paddy shudder. He decided that he didn't really have time for this cooking nonsense, so whispered in the ear of a bird at the back of the crowd:

'Can you tell me how I get to England? I need to go home.'

The bird shrugged, giving Paddy a glare for distracting him from his cookery lesson.

Paddy asked another.

'Take the *Euro-star*, dummy!' he replied, scoffing at the apparent ridiculousness of Paddy's question.

Paddy slumped. There was no way he was going back on the train, after his recent escapade. With that in mind, he spoke louder, towards a few birds in the crowd, to see if they would offer a more helpful response. Again, he was laughed off.

By now, the pigeon chef on the podium had overheard Paddy's accent moving through the crowd.

'Hey! English! Come over here!' she said. 'Maybe I can help'.

---

[11] Birds are rather flammable creatures, so any trouble with fire can escalate *pretty* quickly. SIDENOTE TO ALL HUMAN READERS: DO NOT TRY THIS RECIPE AT HOME

The crowd of pigeons turned to face Paddy, curious of the lost foreigner in their land, but also visibly peeved at the interruption to their cookery show. Paddy felt naked. Well technically, he already was. Birds usually are. But now he felt figuratively naked, metaphorically exposed, as well as literally.

'Come up here, don't worry. I won't bite'. The chef beckoned Paddy towards her.

The crowd parted like the red sea, creating a pathway for Paddy to walk up to the raised platform. He hated being in public, but being in public in another country, was another matter. Unthinkable.

Paddy half-expected a barrage of insults to fly at him as he made his way up the steps. Instead, an impatient silence snapped at his heels. Thirty pairs of eyes were following his every move with great intrigue. The last thing Paddy wanted to do was ruin the chef's recipe.

He felt his insides go all wobbly, and had a recipe of his own, brewing in his stomach. The current mix of ingredients in there were a concoction of nerves and vulnerability, swirled together with the trolley snacks he'd eaten on the Eurostar. It wouldn't be appetising to anyone.

The chef could sense Paddy's unease.

'Okay, that's enough for today, class dismissed!' She called out. 'Next week we'll be working on our crème brulees. To avoid any fiery accidents, don't bring anything silly, like blowtorches or flamethrowers or other incendiary items that you've picked up in the gutter somewhere; pocket lighters only please'.

The crowd slowly parted, somewhat surprised by the sudden ending to their lesson. Half of them were trying to eavesdrop on Paddy, while others were making mental recipe notes for the next session.

'And you there', the chef called to one member of the crowd, a local pigeon who was still watching Paddy intently. 'Stop staring at the foreigner. He's just like us – make him welcome'.

The chef apologized to Paddy, on behalf of the staring bird, before introducing herself officially:

'Enchanté! I am Mademoiselle Michelle Michel, the first pigeon chef to be awarded 3 golden feathers in the world of avian cuisine.'

Paddy looked blank.

'3 golden feathers means I'm good. *Really* good. The best of the best, and most significantly, better than the men. 2 feathers is all the best of the men has mustered. For years they got all the prizes. However, my work is so undeniably exceptional, it has trumped them all. Okay, I'll stop bragging. But you want to know my secret?'

'I just want to know how to get back…'

'I waste nothing', Michelle interrupted, and continued: 'even the most disgusting rubbish can be turned into something exquisite. For example, cigarette ash for smokiness, stale beer for some depth, chewing gum for texture, wild herbs, grasses and weeds for a kick. It's all gravy, baby'.

Paddy couldn't get a word in edgewise.

'Here, English, meet my friends', Michelle said. She called to the other side of the street: 'Alex, Thierry, come on up here'. They nodded in turn, and made their way over the road and up the steps.

Thierry was the older of the two. He had clearly seen better days, and had fading grey feathers. He had a gammy leg, which actually appeared to give him some swagger, as he limped towards the podium. Alex, on the other hand, was a young bundle of energy, and nearly got himself run over in excitement.

Alex introduced himself first.

'Enchanté. Je m'appelle Alex. And this here is Thierry. What's your name?

'Paddy. Enchanté…to you too'.

'Bonjour Paddy' Thierry said, smiling weakly, as if something deep down had been troubling him, but he didn't want to show it.

Michelle Michel butted back in.

'Thierry used to be the happiest bird alive, back in the day, until he lost his one true English love. Then he forgot how to love. Now he's a bit of a grump. We always say that the Morrigan has taken his heart from him, because he doesn't use it anymore. We still think he's loveable though, don't we Alex. Well, sort of.'

'Thank you for your *generous* introduction', Thierry said sarcastically, 'although I'm sure Paddy knows that stories about the Morrigan aren't true'. Thierry proceeded to light a cigarette stub that he found on the pavement, with a lighter he kept under his wing.

'Those stories are true!' Paddy said. 'The Morrigan told me herself that she borrows the hearts and souls of birds who fail to use them. I met her in London right before I came here'.

'Oh dear Paddy, you really are as naïve as you look aren't you'. Michelle said.

'No really! I met the guardians of the...'

Michelle cut him off again. Perhaps her abruptness came from years of working in French kitchens, where there is no place whatsoever for idle talk. She went on:

'Meanwhile, Alex here, is a major leader in the birdy fashion world. Always dreaming of becoming a peacock, aren't you darling'.

'Oui, Oui, indeed. Peacock-chic is my style', Alex said. He gave a twirl of his brightly coloured outfit, which had been woven into his natural pigeon feathers.

'You look very fashionable, Alex', Paddy said earnestly. 'I didn't know birds could dress like that!'

'We have some work to do with you then, don't we', Alex winked.

'I would love to stay', Paddy said. 'I really would, but I need to get home to England. I'm trying to get to pigeon paradise. Trafalgar Square, in London.'

'Pigeon paradise?' Michelle said. 'Well, that works with us. We can be a team, like the three musketeers, except with four'.

'Wh-what do you mean? You want to come to England too?' Paddy said.

Michelle gave Paddy another pitying look, before replying: 'Earlier, I saw you come out from Gare du Nord. I heard you asking some of my students how to get back to England. I realised that you must have arrived by Eurostar, so I invited you up here, because, by a wonderful coincidence, Alex, Thierry and myself have been planning a trip to England for *months*. Who better to plan a trip to England with than a real English pigeon! And now we know that it is actually possible for a bird to travel by Eurostar! We'll simply take the train home with you. It is as if the stars have aligned in our favour. We all have our own reasons for going, you see. I am going to take over the food scene, Alex is going to rock the fashion industry and Thierry is going to return to his one true English love. The thing I'm dying to know is – how did you do it? How did you get past the guards? How did you survive the train journey unseen? What you've done is truly a miracle. I would give up all of my best cooking tips to know your secret.'

'I want to go back', Paddy said. 'But it's not that simple, and there's no way I'm going on Eurostar again. I was seen, and at one point thought I was dead. I pooped in somebody's bag and it was the most traumatic experience of my entire life.'

'What type of bag was it? Louis? Chanel?' Alex asked, with immense interest.

'You pooped in someone's bag?' Michelle said. 'That sounds terrible, but kind of badass; I wasn't expecting that from you. Well at least you came out of it unscathed. You just can't trust those humans, can you, especially in the cities. It's like they've forgotten about nature altogether. Birds were here long before people, you know. What do you think, Thierry? You're the only one who's tried to go to England before'.

Thierry furrowed his brow. 'I think Eurostar is risky. The staff will be extra vigilant after the Paddy situation, and you never know, they might even be carrying guns. Most people would be delighted to see a pigeon burst into a thousand feathers, I bet. If we can't go by Eurostar, the alternative is to fly to Calais, and cross the channel to Dover. But we won't get across the border easily. The seagulls keep the French in France, and the English in England'.

'What are you talking about?' Alex asked.

'Border police', Michelle said. 'Supposedly, there's not enough grain to go around for birds to migrate willy-nilly any more. That's why, in my cooking, I like to make the most of very little, to show that it's possible for us all to share, and enjoy'.

'There must be another way', Paddy said insistently.

'I'm afraid not, little bird', Thierry said. 'Nobody has been known to get past the seagulls. I tried once, many years ago'.

'He doesn't like talking about it', Michelle said. 'He tried to visit his girlfriend in England once, but was unsuccessful. How about it though Thierry, we could try one more time? Surely you would do anything to see your love once again'.

'I'm not even sure she's still there', Thierry said. 'I gave it my all the last time I tried. But the seagulls outfoxed me. I snuck onto a fisherman's boat, but the patrolling birds above discovered me, and it must have been twenty of them that sunk their beaks into my feathers and pulled me out. Not only did I not make it, I had broken bones and my body was in pieces, tattered and bloody. I was ready for the crows to come and take me'.

'But they didn't!' Paddy said. 'And now you're recovered, surely it's worth another shot'. Paddy felt a surge of courage course through his veins. The Morrigan's powers were surely starting to present themselves. He was convinced of it, even if his new friends thought of the queen of crows only as a myth.

Thierry gave it some thought. He seemed to respect Paddy's determination.

'If we're going to do it, we'll need to head to the Champs Elysée first. Air traffic control for birds. They should be able to help with directions. Now, we could take the underground metro there, or - '

Paddy glowered at the suggestion of getting another train.

'Flying it is', Thierry concluded.

'Champs Elysée', Paddy said. 'Sounds fancy.'

'It is fancy, and has a rich history', Thierry said. 'Did you know for instance, that Elysée comes from the Greek word Elysium, which actually means paradise'.

'Huh. Well, I guess we'll be going from one paradise to another', Paddy said, amazed by the miraculous coincidence of paradise in a place, that before today, he'd never even known.

7

The four musketeers: Thierry, Michelle Michel, Alex, and Paddy, all arrived at the Champs Elysée within minutes of agreeing to embark on their daring adventure. Thierry, the old wise head, had led the way, flowing through the Parisian streets with more ease than the river Seine.

En route, chef Michelle Michel had rustled up a packed lunch for the journey ahead, which included: frogs legs, snails, and a mixture of seeds. It definitely sounds a lot worse than it actually was.

Fashionista Alex meanwhile, gathered all the brightly coloured feathers he could find, and put them into a sack (well, a small carrier bag to you and me), which he carried from his beak. He would need the feathers to look his best for London's fashion scene.

And Paddy, looking around at his new friends, with every passing moment, felt increasingly confident in his powers of courage. He had no doubt that he and his French companions would make it to London, one way or another.

'So what happens next?' Paddy asked Thierry, as they touched down next to a sycamore tree.

'We must find a navigation specialist. These birds help guide other birds to travel long distances'.

'But I thought you'd done this trip to Calais before', Paddy said. Why would we need outside help?'

'It is true – I did attempt this trip, once, a long time ago'. Thierry said, with a sigh, as he contemplated his long-lost, English lady pigeon love. 'But if you remember, I failed in my attempt to get past the seagulls and cross the channel. The gulls view migrating birds as a threat to their share of the grain. And now that their control of the borders has strengthened, they won't let anyone through if they don't like the look of them. If we're to be successful, this time we'll need some assistance, preferably from a starling – they are communications experts, and professional bird smugglers. Starlings can send a tweet faster than the wind, and have useful connections in all sorts of unexpected places. Hopefully, they will arrange for our safe passage, hidden away from the border patrolling seagulls'.

Paddy soon became aware that there were many starlings in the area, talking hurriedly to small groups of birds. Paddy knew now that this was the real reason they were at the Champs Elysée. Any sightseeing would have to wait for another trip. There was serious work to do.

Paddy found out from Thierry that the collective noun for starlings is a murmuration, and boy oh boy, were these birds murmuring. Gossipy chirps and scandalous witterings were being exchanged at a ferocious speed.

Paddy was convinced he'd even overheard some vicious rumours being spread about his celebrity parents, but he did his best to shut the noise out.

One starling looked particularly animated, but spoke in the faintest whisper. She looked like she was trying to sell something; something fishy, something *illegal*. Paddy listened in:

'For a bag of grain, I'll tell you how to get to Germany. For 5 bags of grain, Russia. For 50 bags of grain, I'll get you into North Korea'.

This starling was clearly one of the professional bird smugglers that Thierry had just been describing.

'That's Nadia', Thierry said, pointing at the starling that Paddy had overheard. 'She's the best at what she does, but expensive. If we can spare some of our food, she should help us'.

Nadia looked shifty, as though she was protecting dark secrets. She seemed like a tough nut to crack. The four musketeers approached with caution, hoping to covertly grab her attention.

Thierry discreetly caught Nadia's ear, and whispered his request. He didn't want the plans to be overheard by other birds, least of all, any spying seagulls.

Nadia then beckoned the others closer, before uttering her response:

'To get to Calais, that's half a bag of grain. But to England? I can't make any guarantees there. Unless you had some serious grain to exchange'.

'We don't have much at all', Thierry said. 'But we do have Michelle Michel, the finest pigeon chef in the world. She will cook you something so delicious, right now, that you will find it impossible to refuse our offer'.

'Bah! Are you mad? We starlings only trade in grain. How dare you waste my time? I bid you goodbye'.

Nadia turned to face the other way, and was shaking her head at Thierry's seemingly unsatisfactory offer. She proceeded to look for new customers.

Yet before she scooted off, an enticing smell made its way to her nostrils.

In the background, Michelle Michel had been quietly cooking up a storm.

It sent Nadia into a stupor. She was so intoxicated by the smell of the food that she started dancing uncontrollably.

'Give me some of that. NOW!' She demanded.

'Just a taster', Thierry said, and gave her a spoonful of the delicious broth Michelle had made.

Nadia sipped. 'It's glorious, magnificent – a party on the tongue. It's driving me quackers.' She was drunk with joy.

'Now', Thierry said. 'We can give you the rest, if *you* can arrange safe passage for us to England'.

'Okay', Nadia said, reconsidering her offer. 'I'm sure we can reach a deal. You must follow me so that I can give you detailed instructions in private. We must do it out of sight of any suspecting birds. Especially seagulls'.

Nadia led them into a dark alley. Paddy started to have a grim feeling, as though the Morrigan were close by.

Once they were all huddled together in the quiet, Nadia continued the conversation:

'So you want to go to England, eh? I tell you, few journeys are more treacherous than this one. I have made difficult journeys myself. I am from Algeria originally, and migrated North to France for the cooler temperatures. All that climate change is really spicing things up in North Africa, you know. Thousands of birds are fleeing with their families, to try and reach Europe, but it's nearly impossible. The seagulls along the coastline keep saying there's not enough grain to go around, so they've closed off the borders. That's why us starlings deal in grain; we're stockpiling, because we've got no idea what might happen in the future. Obviously exceptions can be made to our usual way of business, if you keep giving me some of that tasty broth'.

Nadia took another sip, and nodded in approval at Michelle Michel.

'Ah, ma cherie!' Michelle said. 'Thank you for the compliment on my cooking (although I don't need really need anybody to tell me how great it is). Don't worry yourself. There'll be plenty of grub for your North African friends, and indeed all birds. We just have to learn how to use it creatively so that everyone gets a share'.

'Well you've just proved that it's possible to me now', Nadia said, licking the remaining bits of soup from her beak. 'You best make some more for me when you return. Anyway, here are your directions'. Nadia pulled out a map, showing the way to Calais, the border crossing.

'When you get to Calais, you will stay with my friend Zizou. He owns a nest in a secret warehouse by the port. We will send word of your arrival to him before you get there, and he will provide more specific directions when you get close. When you meet him, you see nothing, hear nothing, speak nothing. Understand?'

The four musketeers were a bit taken aback by the level of secrecy needed for this operation. The situation with the seagulls must have been even worse than they thought.

'Understand?' Nadia repeated, with a threatening look in her eye.

'Er - oui, oui', the pigeons said, nodding earnestly.

'Whatever you do, don't deviate from the plan', Nadia warned. 'You could get us all in a lot of trouble, which may end in your swift demise, and a visit from the queen of crows. Remember, we have eyes, ears and beaks everywhere, and you wouldn't want us reporting you into the gulls, would you'.

The pigeons all looked rather terrified.

'Good. So ensure you follow my instructions to the letter'.

'Wh-why is everything so secretive?' Paddy asked.

'Give me some more soup and I'll tell you a little something'. Michelle offered another spoonful.

'Between you and me, Zizou is hiding thousands of foreign migrant birds, who the seagulls would thoroughly disapprove of, if they knew they were all in France. Zizou provides shelter for them until they can find a safe route somewhere. Now that's all you're getting, and you didn't hear that from me! And don't attract too much attention. I'm looking at you, Alex'.

If birds could blush, Alex would have done. His brightly coloured peacock outfit would have to be concealed for this flight. He quickly stuffed his vibrant feathers in his sack, so that he blended in with his grey friends.

Nadia swiped the remains of Michelle Michel's food, to make sure that both sides of the negotiation were satisfied, and escorted the four pigeons back out into the wintry light.

Instantly, and without warning, a murmuration of starlings surrounded them, helping them to prepare for their trip to Calais. The starlings fluttered together in a synchronous dance, setting up everything for the flight ahead.

'What's all this about?' Paddy asked.

'Air traffic control for birds', Thierry replied. 'These starlings have the latest technology. A weather vane made from twigs, a control tower (aka the arc de triomphe), and a wind sock, which is actually just a dirty old human sock (it's a bit smelly, but it works)'.

Weather reports were then called out by individual starlings:

'Wind speed: 6 knots'

'Wind direction: Northerly'

'Conditions: Overcast, with a hopeful smattering of blue sky'.

And then a final call from Nadia: 'Now go, pigeon friends. While you still have light. Bon voyage!'

The four musketeers exchanged glances to say they were ready. They flapped furiously, and off they went, rushing through the air above the tree-lined boulevard, eventually soaring right through the arc de triomphe at one end, as if it were a starting gate. The clock was ticking to the end of the day.

They climbed above the Champs Elysée, above the cars and lampposts and buildings that lined the avenue. The arc de triomphe continued shrinking in size as the birds climbed higher and higher, right until it looked, from afar, as tiny as a bird.

8

Traversing the boundary between humankind and nature, the pigeons left behind the concrete jungle of Paris and entered a countryside of green and gold. Their bird's-eye views gave them unique perspectives over the land. Soaring high over the farms and fields, they looked down at the many trapezia joined together like a grassy patchwork blanket.

At their altitude, they encountered all sorts of objects that are often missed at ground level. Planes, gliders, kites, hot air balloons, not to mention countless other birds, all going their own ways.

They even saw some man-made birds. Robotic, humourless helicopters. Drones, to you and me, but to the four musketeers, they looked like evil mutant birds of prey. Luckily, they didn't attack.

Avoiding all these wondrous objects, the pigeons whistled through mist and cloud, as the sun sagged its way down towards the horizon. Nadia had assured them that, so long as they made it before dark, everything would be fine. But, they were losing light rapidly. If the sun disappeared, they'd be lost, and out in the cold.

The pigeons fast approached Calais, and looked for signs of the bird smuggler Zizou or his warehouse. Yet they had no idea what to look out for. It was all top secret stuff, and Nadia, Zizou's confidante, hadn't given them much to go on.

Some 10 miles out from the port, the pigeons encountered a lone starling, which flew above them in the opposite direction. It was very odd for a starling to be alone up here, they thought. Starlings normally stay close to their murmuration, their troupe of synchronised dancers. So, was this lone bird, just possibly, the mysterious Zizou?

Then, the starling did something even more unusual. It flew straight above the pigeons, as if it hadn't even noticed them.

Apparently, this wasn't Zizou. This bird was probably just a lost soul trying to get back to murmuring with the rest of his crew.

However, as the starling breezed overhead, something glinted in the air.

A silver piece of paper began falling miraculously through the sky, shining as it caught the light. It looked like it could have been a sign. Although saying that, *all* shiny things, in fact, look like signs of great importance to pigeons.

In any case, Thierry called out: 'grab it, quick!'[12]

As the paper was carried by the wind, it danced left and right, slipping through the beaks of Alex, Michelle and Thierry, and was plummeting down towards the Earth. Paddy knew it was down to him to recover the paper. *He* was flying below the others, so was the last rung on the ladder, the last hope of capturing the sign. After Paddy it would be only air, nothingness, and loss.

Paddy thought of his daring mother, MTM, who would have relished moments like this. His brain clicked into gear and he began beating his wings against the wind, to try and catch the silvery paper.

Paddy soon disappeared, behind a mass of cloud. Seconds turned into minutes. He was at the mercy of the elements.

As the others began fearing for Paddy's safety, they debated what to do. Should they look for him? Or fly on the same course? They opted to do the latter.

And right they were. Paddy returned triumphantly, with the paper in his beak. He was breathless after his sprint, but the powers of courage had aided him just when he needed them, right when he took the decision to be brave.

The other birds breathed a collective sigh of relief, before agreeing to look at the paper together. They changed their flying formation so that they could all see at the same time. They took great care not to drop it with the wind blasting in their faces.

They looked down at the paper, and inspected it closely.

The paper was a silver rectangle shape, with nothing but a symbol: a yellow asterisk.

What did it mean?

It could have been a message from Zizou, but it seemed unlikely. There were no directions. Was this even meant for the four musketeers? Maybe they should have just let the piece of paper fall to the ground.

They decided to fly below the cloud, so they could see more birds – perhaps one of them would be Zizou, or even a messenger. However, light was fast fading, and the pigeons' feathers looked like camouflage against the grey sky.

Thierry started to look glum, as if the plan had already failed. He looked like he was starting to give up on his English romance once again.

---

[12] Even the most seasoned birds get distracted by glittering objects. They're hard-wired for it.

'Don't worry', Alex said. 'We'll figure it out. Love always wins, in the end'.

It wasn't much comfort to Thierry, who had already lost in love many times before. For an old bird like him, he didn't have much time left. He had already accepted that if they didn't find Zizou, the whole trip would fail.

Nevertheless, the others urged him onwards, praying that they would get to Calais soon.

Paddy was now imagining, a little unrealistically, that they were about to be greeted by a friendly concierge, who would escort them to Zizou's warehouse, wrapping them up in blankets, feeding them shortbread biscuits and steaming hot cups of tea. Only fancy pigeons, like his dad, ever got that sort of treatment. But he was long gone now.

And as the sun dipped behind the edge of the world, everyone's disappointment was replaced by panic. If they didn't find Zizou soon, they would have to find food and shelter of their own.

Paddy gazed down at thousands of small white strips which covered a huge patch of land.

'It's a mass grave, Paddy', Thierry said, seeing that Paddy looked puzzled. 'It's for the soldiers that died in a human war, a long time ago'.

A mass grave, Paddy thought. He felt shivers. The Morrigan, queen of crows and gatekeeper to the birdy underworld, suddenly re-entered his mind.

'I think I see it! The warehouse.' Michelle said.

'See what?' Alex said.

'What are you talking about? We haven't seen any birds', Thierry said.

Michelle replied smugly: 'What you're all missing, is that we're not supposed to meet a bird in the air. We're supposed to meet a bird on the ground'.

She nodded her head down, and sure enough, right below them, was a gigantic, ashy coloured building with a yellow asterisk on top. The warehouse.

Finally, they had made it. Whoops and cheers and high-fives went around, as they descended towards their target.

While the others were celebrating however, Thierry was typically cautious: he didn't want to show signs of his optimism, even though inside he started to feel a sense of blazing anticipation, a burning love. Every flap of his wings was taking him a few inches closer to being reunited with his English girlfriend. Assuming he could get across the border, of course. And also assuming that he would find her, amongst the thousands of pigeons in London. But that could wait until later.

Squinting into the dusk, the pigeons could make out a metallic black starling, lurking in the shadows of one of the rear entrances. If it got any darker, he'd be completely invisible. The perfect disguise I suppose, for a bird smuggler.

The four musketeers closed in, and a thought occurred to Paddy: just how many foreign birds was Zizou was concealing in this massive place?

The starling looked suspicious of the travellers, and pretended to mind his own business, while he waited for one of the pigeons to initiate the conversation. A thick silence swelled in the air.

Paddy plucked up the courage to break it. 'Hello', he said. 'It's Zizou, right?'

'You see nothing. You hear nothing. You speak nothing. Understand?'

He turned on his heel and dashed into the warehouse. The four musketeers looked at each other blankly, unsure if this really was the bird in question.

The starling popped his head back out. 'Don't just stand there, you fools! Come in. Unless you want to be made into a birdy soup for the seagulls'.

'Eugh – if only the gulls had some taste, I could make them a delicious soup with all that extra grain they're hoarding. It would be much less messy', Michelle scoffed. The pigeons did their best to suppress their chuckling, but the odd squeak still escaped.

'This is no laughing matter', the starling said sternly. 'The gulls have locked down the borders, and locked down the grain. This is a crisis for many birds and their families, who have been separated from their homelands and communities. Follow me'.

Once they were out of sight, in the dry and the warm of the warehouse, the starling quietly introduced himself properly.

'Welcome. I am Zizou. I offer you a room for the night, and the best advice I can give on getting you to England. But I cannot make promises. The gulls have sold their souls to the Morrigan in exchange for control of the birdy borders, and naturally, the grain'.

'Sold their souls? But the Morrigan is not real', Michelle said. Alex and Thierry nodded in agreement.

'You'd be a fool to doubt it. The gulls have this coastline controlled with an iron fist. Gone are the days of free movement of birds'.

'See! I told you!' Paddy whispered, feeling vindicated. 'It's just like the Morrigan told me, she takes the hearts and souls of birds who no longer use them'.

'Too right', Zizou said. 'And these seagulls are the most heartless, soulless creatures in the animal kingdom. Worse even than humans, dare I say it'.

The pigeons began bickering amongst themselves about whether the Morrigan truly existed.

'Hush'. Zizou said. 'You see nothing. You hear nothing. You speak nothing. Understand?'

Zizou led them behind a curtain, and into one of the building's vents. They shuffled through blackened corridors, hardly able to see, for what felt like forever. The vent must have been a mile long, around the outer perimeter of the building.

Zizou took the pigeons past many families, shadowy groups of birds: faceless, nameless and voiceless, displaced and apparently unaccepted by the local gulls.

They must have passed hundreds of such birds before they reached their designated nesting spot, which was situated near an exit vent on the far side of the warehouse.

'You sleep here. Understand?' Zizou said, as he laid a black cloth down, to be used as a shared bird blanket for the four of them. 'Before dawn, head out through this vent. Ensure that you leave before sunrise - that's when the seagulls wake up and start their border patrol shift. You have a narrow window to get across the channel to England with enough light so that you can see but not so much light that you are seen. That, I'm afraid, is the best you can hope for in these troubling times. Now, go to sleep. I don't want a peep from any of you. Disturb me at your peril. I can call the Morrigan at a moment's notice, and she will see to you'.

The four musketeers thanked Zizou, and understood the challenge that awaited them tomorrow. How was it possible to see and not be seen? There was only one way to find out.

Paddy was exhausted. He'd already accomplished more today than his entire life so far. But before he could revisit the events in his mind, he collapsed into the makeshift nest, under cover of darkness. This time though, he was wrapped in a darkness of security, rather than the captivity of the train's upturned bin. He slept like a log.

9

A cacophony of chirping brought in the new day. On a regular morning, this would have been a delightful thing to wake up to. But on this day, it was a truly disastrous thing to hear, because it meant that the pigeons had missed the crack of dawn. They were late.

The gulls, aka the birdy border patrol force, would be starting their shift right away, if they hadn't already, and the pigeons' brief window of opportunity to cross the channel undetected would be closing. Imminently.

Unfortunately, the pigeons had slept a little too well in Zizou's warehouse, and none of them had had the luxury of an alarm clock to wake them on time. Admittedly, it was a fairly major flaw in their otherwise perfect plan. While the birds around them were twittering away joyously, the four musketeers were all a panicked flurry of feathers, as they anxiously bundled out of the vent at the rear of the warehouse.

They were greeted by the smell of the salty air, and the sound of the nearby cries of the seagulls, who were wide-awake, and patrolling.

'Sacre bleu!' Alex said. 'How are we going to get past them?'

'Don't you worry, I'll show them who's le chef around here', said Michelle Michel, clenching imaginary fists.

'Brute force won't work, Michelle. We're outnumbered here', Thierry said. 'The original plan no longer works for us'.

'Do…we have a plan B?' Paddy enquired, looking hopefully at the others.

'Not exactly a plan B. More like a plan Z', Thierry said gravely. 'If this doesn't work, there aren't any more letters in the alphabet that can save us'.

'Come on, spit it out then, Thierry, what is it?' Michelle demanded.

'We're going to take cover on the passenger ferry, and cross the channel with the humans'.

'Im-possible', Michelle said.

'*Im-possible*', Alex said.

'Impossible', Paddy said.

Thierry was unswayed, looking around at the others for any bright ideas: 'What other choice do we have? I'm serious.' He found only unconvinced faces. This was the first time that Thierry had been doubted, for even though they had come so far, they still remained in France. Yet Thierry pressed on, trying to persuade them: 'We can use the feathers in Alex's sack to hide under, so long as he has a choice of colours other than neon pink'.

'How dare you accuse me of such a narrow colour palette, Thierry. In fact, I have many classic styles, which will blend in nicely with the white decking of the boat. Just because I'm pushing the boundaries of fashion, it doesn't mean I forget my roots. Now, if you'll all take a look at this, there could be hope for us yet'. Alex opened the carrier bag to show a full spectrum of colour and a wealth of accessories, which could be combined to form millions of designs.

Thierry nodded in approval, and gave Alex an apologetic smile.

Slowly but surely, the others became increasingly optimistic in the last-ditch plan. As Thierry had said, what other choice did they have?

'Follow me', Thierry said, with renewed self-confidence. He had a sense of déjà vu, as he remembered the Calais roads from the last time he attempted the cross-channel journey. The map in his head was revealing itself at just the right time. He took them through the narrow streets towards the shore, ensuring that they didn't arouse any suspicion.

Each time a seagull flew overhead, the pigeons ducked for cover in a front porch or under the awning of a shop. Each time, they were shooed away by the early-risers (otherwise known as the crazy morning people) setting up for the day. With every seagull cry, Paddy felt the deathly spirit of the Morrigan wash over him, but his powers of courage forced him to press on, which encouraged the others to do the same.

Arriving at the port, the four musketeers perched behind cars on the ramp leading into the boat. Seagulls could be heard everywhere, but not seen. The foghorn of the ferry blasted. It was due to leave.

'It's perfect', Paddy said.

'Next stop, England', Michelle said gleefully.

They made a dash for the boat, flying with all their might to reach the ship's deck, unseen. Of course, they couldn't hide in with the humans. They'd be kicked out faster than a flying birdpoo.

The train fog-horned again. It sounded like a troll burping.

The pigeons made it to the deck, so far unscathed. They manically flapped around, reaching into Alex's bag of feathers for camouflage.

Another booming sound rang out from near the boat. It sounded like the foghorn but deeper. More sinister.

It rang again, the second time more clearly.

'Hold it right there', it called.

Time moved slow as the realisation kicked in that they'd been spied…by seagulls.

'Where do you think you're off to?' A scruffy and mangy seagull squawked, as it swooped down onto the decking, joined by several others.

The gulls had begun their inquisition.

'We're going to England', Paddy said, stoutly.

'Well you do sound pretty English to me. What do you think boss?'

The tattered gull turned to his commander-in-chief, whose feathers were, by contrast, shiny and conditioned. The chief was a flabby sort of bird, overfed and unhealthy but excessively pampered. He had a pompous and sneering air, too. He clearly had great power and wealth, but Paddy couldn't fathom how he'd acquired it.

The chief looked satisfied that Paddy was English. There was no denying it. His accent and his awkward stance told the gulls all they needed to know.

'How about your companions?' the chief asked, looking at the French birds.

'They are English too!' Paddy insisted.

'They…can speak for themselves', the chief said. He was starting to take control.

Alex was up first, and put on his best British accent.

'I'm a proper country bird, I am', Alex said hopefully.

'That', the boss said, 'is the worst British accent I have ever heard. Ever. And you two? Speak up'.

A heavy silence hung on the others. If Alex couldn't convince them, Michelle and Thierry didn't have a chance.

'The three of *us* are French' Thierry said, making a distinction between Paddy and the rest of them. 'Is there a problem?'

'Damn bleedin' right there's a problem. We've got enough problems as it is without you extras coming in. Not enough grain in England for more birds. So you lot will have to go back. Apart from him', he said, pointing at Paddy. 'I don't know how on Earth you got here lad, but you'll be going right back to Blighty on this here ferry'.

'Where you have you all come from anyway. Where are they hiding all the others?'

'All the others? I'm afraid I have no idea what you're talking about', Thierry said.

'Don't act all ignorant. I know there's some dodgy bird smuggling going on around here somewhere, I can almost smell the stench of the thousands of mucky birds in their secret den. Regardless, they didn't fool us this time did they'. The chief smirked.

'This is unfair', Thierry said, nearly welling up. 'I want to speak to the bird in charge of all this'.

'Funny you should say that. You're speaking directly to him. Moi', he said, puffing up his chest proudly. 'I am the right honourable Trumpus Sauvage, birdy patrol border chief, leader of the sea gullies, protector of the avian realms of England and France, lordy overlord of grain, commander of the English channel and all things England, and'

'All right, I get it', Thierry said tetchily. 'That's enough'.

Trumpus Sauvage looked so shocked at Thierry's effrontery, that he was lost for words. Thierry didn't seem affected by Mr. Trumpus' titles whatsoever.

'Listen, Mr. Sauvage, I will be straight with you. If you're a decent enough bird to hear me out to me for one minute, I will explain a few of the compelling reasons why you should allow us into your fine country'.

'Go on then', Mr. Sauvage said.

'Firstly, the lady to my right, Michelle Michel, is the greatest pigeon chef in France, and I suspect, the world.' Michelle nodded furiously in agreement. 'She is an expert in using grain more efficiently, so that twice as many birds can eat with half the amount of grain. Not only that, if you allow her to cook for you right now, she will cook you the most delicious food you've ever eaten in your life'.

Trumpus turned his nose up. He didn't like the sound of French food, least of all that it would be made by a lady. Nevertheless, he listened.

'Alex, to my left, is the finest fashion designer in Paris. With his clothing, he keeps more birds warm than ovens at Christmas. He gives other birds confidence to be the best version of themselves, through his landmark collection 'peacock-chic', and has even developed a material to protect birds against predators. I assure you that every bird in England, yourself included, would welcome his skills'.

'And you?' Trumpus asked.

'I am here for love. Simply love. No more and no less. I am an old bird, but I hold inside a passion so strong that it must be shared with my one, the bird who was the love of my youth and, since we were parted many years ago, has been the love of my dreams'.

'So you're telling me that a cook, a pretend peacock and a wrinkly old lover deserve a place in England?'

'Well, yes'.

'Bahahahahaha. You're out of your mind. You're coming off this boat straightway and I'm sending you three to the loonybin. Let's go, the lot of yer'.

Trumpus Sauvage signalled to his henchmen (or henchbirds, rather), who immediately swarmed the French pigeons. In spite of fierce resistance from the pigeons, who clawed and bit at the gulls, they were finally overpowered. In the end, it took nearly ten gulls to each pigeon to prise them off the boat and carry them back to shore.

Paddy was left with a few of the underling seagulls, whose job was to take him to England.

Paddy was devastated. Even knowing that he'd be going back home wasn't enough to cure the loss of his new friends. And knowing that Thierry wouldn't be united with his English love - that was the greatest injustice of all. Paddy began cursing the powers of courage, for leading them to the seagulls, but it was too late now. Why would the Morrigan give him powers that led to failure? It didn't make sense.

As he was taken across the channel by the group of pretentious and haughty seagulls, Paddy thought to himself:

'Trumpus Sauvage? Leader of the gullies? What a silly name, and what a silly bunch of birds'.

So, with a raging fire in his belly, Paddy was escorted back to England.

10

'Now go, off with yer', the seagull underling screeched, shooing Paddy off the boat and onto land. 'London's that way'. He pointed to a vague spot in the distance.

Paddy made off in a hurry, eager to get away from the pesky gulls, and perched himself atop the chalky cliffs of Dover; the craggy headland which was his gateway to home. But it was little comfort - the loss of his friends made him feel more alone than ever. He trudged off, aiming for the general direction of London, but soon lost the will to fly, once he was out of the clutches of the birdy border patrol.

The seagulls seemed to have turned their attention elsewhere, anyway. They continued to bark commands along the border, ordering each other to watch for any incoming birds that weren't their own kind.

Of course, after the pigeons' recent failure, there wouldn't be any other birds crazy enough to try the crossing. Everything was already on lockdown. Trumpus Sauvage was conducting a ruthlessly efficient operation.

It got Paddy thinking, didn't the gulls have anything better to do? What were they going to do with all this excess grain they were hoarding? They were all fat enough as it was. But it was little consolation to Paddy.

He continued for a couple of miles, hanging his head in despair and commiseration - for his French companions first and foremost – but also, for himself, for having been separated from them.

Disappointment was replaced by emptiness as he marched inland. He would have to muster up the energy to fly soon, but he couldn't manage it yet.

Regardless of what had happened, he still had to pursue his dream of making it to Trafalgar Square. It's what the others would have wanted for him, without a doubt.

A huge flock of new gulls were approaching from over the channel. Hundreds of them. Larger than your regular flock, to be sure. Reinforcements, probably, Paddy thought. He didn't really care anymore. He felt powerless.

The new flock of seagulls soared over the border patrol gullies, and seemed to be trailing Paddy. They looked smaller than usual, and were perhaps the mischievous chicks of Trumpus Sauvage, coming to taunt him.

Paddy simply wanted to be left to his own devices, not to be pestered by these little Sauvage minions. He picked up speed to try and get ahead of them. Talking to them was the least of his concerns.

Despite that, the gulls still tracked his movements, edging closer and closer.

In the end, Paddy couldn't take the stalking any more. He turned and shouted: 'Leave me alone. I don't want to talk to you unless you bring my friends back'.

'We are your friends', the gulls said from afar.

'Yeah, right', Paddy said. He turned his back on them.

'Hey, Paddy, you nicompoop, wait for us'. The abuse was clearly about to start.

Paddy was about to blow his top, and prepared to launch a vicious tirade against the gulls, telling them where to shove their beaks and whatnot, before the seagulls, most concerningly, began getting…*undressed*! In all the madness of the last couple of days, this was the cherry on the cake. Hundreds of birds, taking their clothes off! As each of the birds unpicked themselves feather by feather, they revealed their true forms.

It turns out they weren't gulls at all. These birds were shedding disguises. Many of them were actually pigeons. There were hundreds of them, glorious and grey. There were others too. Starlings, sparrows, finches, even a couple of lapwings. All freed from the tyranny of border patrol, migrating to Britain once more, all for their own important reasons.

Paddy looked for a familiar face among the crowd.

'Hey English', came a familiar call. It was Michelle Michel! Paddy couldn't believe it. He was going to be reunited with his friends. In England.

Paddy rushed over, and his smile widened as he saw Alex and Thierry too.

'How did you do it?' He asked.

'The feathers, obviously. Hadn't you worked that out?' Alex said, chuckling.

'I know, but there are so many birds here – I'm amazed'.

'Well, we did have to pick up some extra feathers from somewhere', Alex said, looking around cheekily at the others. 'After you left, we managed to ambush a few gulls who were isolated from their patrol group, and we plucked them clean. They didn't dare tell on us to Trumpus Sauvage, because they were so embarrassed to be in front of him, in the nude, if you know what I mean. They were as bald as coots by the time we'd finished with them, and by then we had enough white feathers for the whole group - for a whole army of birds dressed as gulls'.

'But surely Trumpus knows by now?'

'Probably. We left him a nice smelly package in his living quarters before we left'.

'All the more reason to be moving quickly on', Thierry said, a look of fiery romance in his eyes.

'Oooh, someone wants to see his girlfriend', Michelle said.

'This is no time for idle joking', Thierry snapped, concerned that some gulls may be spying on them still.

Alex stood up straight, as if addressing a military captain. 'Yes sir!' he said, quickly gathering up the remaining feathers, stuffing them into his sack. Without them, there would be no '*peacock-chic*', the fashion collection he was set to unleash on the streets of London.

And with that, they were bound for London, joined by the other birds who had finally found refuge from the gulls. Many of them were from Zizou's place.

The birds took flight in a wonderfully chaotic formation, and the four musketeers sensed that they were on the home straight.

The morning mist had cleared, and Paddy could have sworn he heard a whisper in the air.

It sounded like the message he'd been told by the Morrigan in the graveyard:

'You must listen to your heart and soul, when your head tells you that something is impossible'.

Paddy's faith in the queen of crows and her powers of courage had been restored. It seemed so clear to him now that he was not the only one who had been blessed with courage. Each and every bird that had crossed the channel had shown great resolve and bravery. It became increasingly obvious that courage was available to all, if one could only find the way to use it.

Trafalgar beckoned, and awaited the courageous.

11

Patrick Jr. R02390 had done more in two days than most birds accomplish in a lifetime.

He had been to Paris (on a train with hundreds of people, I might add), and had navigated his way home via the most treacherous path. He'd shown outstanding courage, thanks in part to the Morrigan, who had supposedly bestowed a special power on him.

At first Paddy had been a bit miffed that the special powers didn't give him abilities like shape-shifting or time-travel, or a powerful laser gun that he could direct with his eyes to destroy his seagull enemies.

After giving it some thought though, he suspected that the Morrigan hadn't given him anything at all; it was possible that she had only brought to Paddy's attention the fact that courage can be called upon from within. The lesson learned was the power in itself.

Even though he and his companions would soon reach Trafalgar, Paddy was certain that the journeys of the rest of their lives were just getting started, and there would be more powers to learn along the way.

When Paddy had set out, his mum had told him to become his own bird, and while he'd conquered his fears, and seen and done things that were barely believable in two days, he still felt like he had a long way to go.

His friends still had a long way to go too:

Alex was preparing to launch his 'peacock-chic' style on the London birdy fashion scene, and who knew how far he could go? Perhaps one day even humans would adopt the look.

Michelle Michel had a lot of work planned as well, to try and feed as many London birds as she could with haute cuisine, thrown together from the littered streets.

By contrast, Thierry's journey was closest to its end - with him being the oldest of the pigeons – yet he was given a late lease of life knowing that his English love could be near. He didn't know for sure that she'd be waiting for him, but he simply had to try and find her. It was romance, after all. Even the oldest and wisest birds are still "becoming" who they are, you know.

When the others had asked Thierry about where he would find her among the thousands of London birds, he replied:

'The last time I saw her, she told me that she'd wait by Nelson's column every day at 12 'o' clock noon until I came back'.

'In Trafalgar Square? Well that's convenient!' Michelle Michel said.

It was convenient indeed, but not hugely surprising. Trafalgar Square was a true haven for lonely pigeons; a bountiful source of food and a secure zone well away from Trumpus Sauvage and the birdy border patrol. A perfect place for love.

Thierry remained cautious however, and mostly kept details about his girlfriend to himself. He hadn't told the other birds more than was absolutely necessary. He didn't want to jinx himself.

Paddy's thoughts meanwhile, turned to home, and he wondered, as he approached London, if his mother had managed to wriggle her way out of the traffic cone in the nest. He hadn't been away long of course, but he hoped that MTM's pizza-free diet would have by now set her free from the confines of the neon-orange plastic trap she was encased in.

Paddy hadn't told the others about his mum. He was a little embarrassed about the whole situation, and besides, it's not very gentlemanly to tell others that your Mum's trying to lose weight. He was sure that his French friends would all meet her in good time.

Darting between the skyscrapers and historic buildings, the flock of birds that had crossed the channel gradually split off on their own paths, ducking into London's alleyways and secret passages, while the pigeons firmly set their sights on Trafalgar Square. Between them, they had enough knowledge to get close.

They flew in sync, in a starling-murmuration sort of way, which moved like a great grey billowing curtain, glistening with metallic green and purple.

Approaching from the East, they descended into the chaotic city. Strings of vehicles lined the streets. Millions of bodies moved below, intermingling.

As they cruised by St. Paul's cathedral, they could at last see the towering statue of Nelson. He was wearing his wide-brimmed hat, just like the old crow had said, and was leaning on his sword. Pigeon paradise was in sight.

Paddy was surprised, and a little abashed by how easy it was to find. The old crow from the graveyard hadn't been lying – it was much easier to find your way around above ground than below.

But of course, Paddy was glad with the way things had turned out, taking the tube instead of the skies. He would never have met Michelle, Alex and Thierry had he taken the easiest route. He would never have learned so much.

The four musketeers finally touched down. They had made it, and it was beyond magical. There were pigeons as far as the eye could see. Paddy felt pride ripple through his wings.

There were street performers, statues, water fountains. Buildings of great importance: embassies, The National Gallery.[13] And most crucially for pigeons, an abundance of food and drink.

Glorious mounds of rubbish and scraps and crumbs and bits and bobs. Paddy and his friends started pecking away furiously, and nearly forgot to take in the fact that they had completed their journey. Even Thierry forgot about his English girlfriend for a while.

They were soon interrupted by the booming chime of Big Ben, which rang all the way down to Trafalgar. The birds counted each bell to see if it was 12 'o' clock noon yet. One, two, three, four…

Thierry spoke, unable to wait.

'I think I see her. My love.'

Alex, Michelle and Paddy looked at each other in half disbelief, half excitement, and by the time they looked back, Thierry was off.

He had barged his way through the crowd, leaving the rest of the musketeers behind. They tried to catch up with him, pushing and shoving their way through, but a little less successfully.

A couple of disgruntled London pigeons shouted 'Oi – what you doing?' as Paddy, Michelle and Alex nudged past.

Their view was blocked by even more birds. All they could hear was Thierry cry out.

'Matilda! Matilda! Oh sweet Matilda'.

It was the first time that the other pigeons had heard Thierry speak her name.

Paddy felt a shiver of strangeness wash over him. He felt the Morrigan's presence nearby.

As the crowd parted in front of Paddy, it revealed two pigeons, desperately in love, kissing and slobbering all over each other.

Thierry and Matilda had been reunited, at last. And they were making up for lost time.

'Mum?!' Paddy called out in bemusement.

---

[13] Even though pigeons weren't allowed in, they still liked the buildings.

Paddy's jaw dropped. It was his Mum, Matilda, MTM, stood in front of him, kissing Thierry with passion. This is gross, Paddy thought.

How had she gotten here? And why was she kissing Thierry? Thierry was much mistaken, surely.

Thierry looked back, just as confused as young Paddy.

Paddy, meet my English love, Matilda, or Mathilde, en francais.

'Meet her? She's my Mum, you numpty, why are you drooling all over her?'

'She's your mother?' Thierry said in utter shock.

'Oh Patrick', Matilda began, 'I don't know how it's possible that you met this bird in France but it is true. I am his long lost love. I fell in love with Thierry before your father, but he was driven out of the country by the birdy border patrol. After many years, I had to try and move on. But I couldn't be happy, especially with that rapscallion father of yours – good riddance to him. Every day I have waited here for my French prince. I never gave up hope'.

Paddy's mind whirred. The pieces slowly came together. *This* was why his Mum had been so miserable with his father, *this* was the reason why she wouldn't let Paddy come down to Trafalgar Square. She had been waiting for Thierry all along.

'I'm sorry I kept it from you all these years', Matilda said, sobbing. 'Thierry. I knew you would never give up'. Her tears became tears of joy.

Paddy understood. His mum was only trying to protect him, and he had never seen her so in love.

Once they'd finished canoodling, Paddy did have a burning question for his mother.

'How did you get out of the cone?'

'A couple of days off the pizza and I wriggled my way out.', Matilda said.

The French birds had blank expressions. They knew nothing about MTM, Matilda's wild alter-ego.

'Another story for later', Paddy said reassuringly.

As they settled in to their new surroundings, a feeling of peace overcame Paddy, and a sense of normality ensued. He looked out across the square.

Alex had begun flaunting his feathers, and was quickly surrounded by birds who wanted a piece of "peacock-chic".

Michelle Michel began rustling up her famous "3 golden-feathered" cuisine, and pigeons instantly flocked to dine in luxury. What started as an orderly queue became a scrum, with birds eager to taste the finest birdy food in London.

Thierry and Matilda took a stroll around Trafalgar, wing-in-wing,[14] catching up on old times, catching up on lost time, and looking forward to the future time they would have together.

Paddy remained still, and pondered the uncanny coincidence of bumping into his mother's long lost boyfriend in France.

Or was it a coincidence? Was this all part of the plan? A plan orchestrated by the Morrigan, queen of crows, gatekeeper to the afterworld? After all, it was her followers who had insisted Paddy take the train. Paddy wanted some sort of a sign to prove it, but it mattered little now. Everybody was where they were supposed to be.

He looked at a puddle on the ground, leftover from the morning's rain. A black shadow swept over it, as if a crow had passed overhead, blocking out the light. Was this the sign of the Morrigan? Would she be coming to rise up out of the murky water to meet him again?

Not today.

The afterlife could wait. For now, Paddy was in paradise.

---

[14] Birds can't hold hands, obviously.

Acknowledgements

Thank you to everyone who has supported me along the way. I am currently working on my second book, and I wouldn't have the freedom to do so without the following people behind me:

Leah Macklin (and the entire Macklin clan)
Johanna Brown
Matthew Cook
Tommy King
My best friends from DCGS and UoL (you know who you are)
The English teachers and professors who made a difference
(special shout-out to Andrew Millar and Clare Birchall)

…and, as goes without saying, all my family.

One final massive thank you to Jill Harrison for her wonderful drawings. Without you I wouldn't have turned this book into something tangible. Here's hoping we can join forces again.